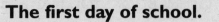
The first day of school.

Now it is the morning of the first day of school and Mrs. Parker is holding up a sack lunch. "I drew a little heart here by your name," she says, smiling. "Is that too embarrassing?"

"Yes," says Agnes. "But I understand that you have to do these mom things."

Mrs. Parker gives her head a little shake and drops a bag full of grapes in the sack. "I can't believe it's already your last year of elementary school!" she says.

"Me neither," says Agnes. She pours herself a bowl of raisin bran and says another little prayer that she and Prejean will be in the same class. She also prays again that she will not, please God, get stuck with Mrs. Libonati. Why can't Neidermeyer get Libbo? And why do these brand-new shoes feel so uncomfortable already? And what if all the girls in the whole class except Agnes show up wearing bras?

OTHER BOOKS YOU MAY ENJOY

AGNeS PARKeR...
GiRl iN PRoGReSS

by Kathleen O'Dell

SCHOLASTIC INC.
New York Toronto London Auckland Sydney
Mexico City New Delhi Hong Kong Buenos Aires

ISBN 0-439-81241-0

12 11 10 9 8 7 6 5   8 9 10/0

Printed in the U.S.A.   40

First Scholastic printing, October 2005

Text set in Berkeley Book
Designed by Kimi Weart

For Tim, Sam, and Charlie, with love

AGNeS PARKeR...
GiRl iN PRoGReSS

CHAPTER ONE

IT IS THE LAST DAY of summer vacation and Agnes Parker is late. She is desperate and pedaling her bike so fast, her socks are falling into her shoes. *Stupid hill . . .* It feels as if the harder she pedals, the slower she goes. And right there, looming in front of her at the top of the slope, is the sign: Hollister Terrace. She leans forward and takes the turn, sticking close to the sidewalk in the shadow of the hulking apartment complex, weaving around the scribbled chalk lines marked out for hopscotch and foursquare.

There are only four and a half more minutes until the start of her favorite TV program, a special Labor Day showing of *Guitar Girls of Planet Z*. She promised

Prejean she will be on time—for sure. And that's why she has dared to take the Hollister Terrace shortcut.

Just two blocks to go. I'm going to make it! thinks Agnes. *I'm going to . . .*

"Haw! Heads up, Gagness!"

Neidermeyer! But where?

"Twelve o'clock!" booms Neidermeyer.

Ka-thwap! Agnes feels a rubbery smack against her head accompanied by a deep echoing *bong!* She wobbles and almost falls off her bike. It's a dodge ball, and Agnes takes it flat on the ear. *Ow, ow, ow . . . Neidermeyer!*

Peggy Neidermeyer is not scary as in *big* and scary. Actually, she is wiry and built like a colt. She has lean, white, muscular shins that are mottled with bruises. Her teeth are small and pointy, kind of like a rat's. And she's a fanatical athlete—captain of nearly every team at nearly every recess.

Neidermeyer has always been the tough one, even in kindergarten, where at every imaginative play session, she commandeered the toy electric shaver. Agnes remembers how she loved to walk around shaving, twisting that chin of hers left and right, talking with one eye squinched up, like Popeye. And even now, in sixth grade, she has not changed much. She is one of the last girls who still loves to sock people.

"And you're out!" Neidermeyer bellows.

Stunned, Agnes looks up. Neidermeyer waggles her

10

tongue and waves from her third-floor balcony. Agnes puts her head down and keeps one hand clapped to her ear all the way to Prejean's house.

"Ohmigosh," says Prejean when she answers the door. "Half your face is all red!"

Agnes points to her flaming earlobe. "Neidermeyer," she says.

"Don't tell me. You took Hollister?" Prejean lifts an eyebrow. "Man, you must have been *late* . . ."

Agnes gives her a tight-lipped smile, kicks off her shoes, and follows her inside (because *nobody* wears shoes on Prejean's mother's perfect carpet). "So how come *you* never get beaned when you take Hollister?" asks Agnes.

"Because," says Prejean, flipping on the TV, "she knows *I'd* try to get her back." She looks over her shoulder and adds, "You're just too known for your . . . niceness."

Agnes thinks this one over. "But I don't *feel* nice. She just makes me so mad, I can't think of anything to say back. I mean, I can see her coming, and I can feel myself getting madder . . ."

"Ooo!" says Prejean. "And she just loves that, you know. She thinks making people mad is so, so funny."

"Yeah," says Agnes. "But then I freeze. Which makes her think I'm just stupid or something."

"Well, luckily, I *don't* freeze. Right?" Prejean gives Agnes's arm a little nudge. "So never fear. Prejean is here."

Somehow her friend's reassurance doesn't exactly make Agnes feel better. "But I want her to know that I'm *not* stupid. In fact," says Agnes, "I'd love it if she could just be a little scared of *me*."

Prejean lifts another eyebrow. "Highly doubtful," she says. "I mean, oh, puh-leez."

Agnes could spend more time being hurt by this remark. But the problem is, Prejean is right. Prejean is practically always right. And then it hits her. Agnes spreads her arms wide and looks up at the ceiling. "Oh, Prejean!" she wails. "What if *this* is the year everything changes?"

"Like what?" says Prejean.

"Like what if *this* is the year they *split us up*?"

"They *can't*," says Prejean. "We're almost sisters. It would be like . . . breaking up Tiff and Zori."

"Hmmmm," says Agnes. Tiff and Zori are interplanetary rock stars with superpowers. She can't picture either of them being split up *or* ka-powed by a dodge ball.

"We'll Super Glue our pants together," says Prejean.

Agnes brightens. "Yes, or we could braid our hair together into one super-connected hairstyle."

"We'll think of *something* . . ." Prejean pounds the floor with her fist. "Darn! This isn't *Guitar Girls*! This is *Dundercat*! I hate *Dundercat*! They changed the stupid schedule."

"That's okay," says Agnes. "I don't think I could even concentrate this morning."

"Maybe we should just call our boyfriends, instead," says Prejean.

"Fabulous!" says Agnes.

Agnes and Prejean have a favorite game. It's a board game with an automated, hot-pink telephone. You use it to talk to boys named Jason. (*Hi. I'm Jason. Want to go to the mall?*) Or Justin. (*This is Justin. Will you be my girl?*) Agnes and Prejean never play by the game's real rules, which have you rolling dice, spinning an arrow, and hopping all over the board in little pastel sports cars. They just like to take the boys' calls. Prejean loves to say, breathlessly, "So, wink-wink, will you treat me like a laaaaaady?" (It is a line from a hilarious late-night movie neither of them were supposed to see.) Agnes, on the other hand, loves to talk to Jason about her boogers. "Sorry, Jason," she says in her most weasily whine. "I can't go to the dance. I've got *booooogers!*"

"It is a wonder that Jaaaason and Justin keep calling baaaaack!" says Agnes in her whiny booger voice.

"But they do, dahling! They can't help themselves!" breathes Prejean.

Agnes and Prejean haven't played the game for a while. When Prejean opens the tidy closet in her lemon-yellow bedroom, they see that the game is perched on the top shelf. "Give me a boost," she says.

Agnes knits her fingers together and makes a stirrup out of her hands. Prejean steps in with her bare foot. "Oof," Agnes says. "You're heavy. Hurry up."

"I'm a growing girl," says Prejean, looking down. She almost loses her balance, and Agnes staggers.

"Help!" says Agnes.

"Hold on," says Prejean, straining to reach as far as she can. Her T-shirt hikes up over her hip, and when Agnes looks up, she is stunned by what she sees.

Prejean hops down holding the game in its pink-and-purple box. "Got it!" she says, hoisting the box in the air like a trophy.

Agnes knows she has a sort of frozen look on her face.

"What's wrong?" says Prejean.

"Shut the door," she says.

Prejean sets down the game. Then she shuts the door softly, turns back to Agnes, and waits.

"Oh, Prejean," says Agnes. "I saw your bra!"

Prejean closes her eyes tightly and then pops them open extra wide. "My *stupid* bra!" she says. "Do you hate me?"

"No, no! Why would I hate you?" asks Agnes.

"Because I know how you always want everything to be the same. Especially us," says Prejean.

Agnes is aware that Prejean has been needing a bra for a while now, but she feels weird talking about it. "I'll get one when I need one," said Agnes. "Which I don't." Agnes busies herself unloading the game from the box.

"I'm sorry," Prejean says. And then there is a silence.

Agnes feels a rush of sympathy. "It's not your fault you're first," she says. "Look, my dodge-balled ear's swelling up. Maybe I could get a little ear-bra and wear it on my head."

Prejean half smiles.

Agnes reaches for the pink plastic phone. "Justin?" says Agnes in a businesslike voice. "Prejean has a stupid bra!" She looks up at Prejean and whispers, "He says hubba-hubba."

Her friend smiles for real and grabs the receiver. "Jason," she says, equally no-nonsense, "Agnes has boogers!"

"But I *wanted* a braaaaaa," whines Agnes.

"But she decided to stick with boooogers," Prejean tells Jason. She covers the phone with her hand. "He's so very relieved, dah-ling. He says he hopes your head is always jam-packed with 'em!"

"Fooorever and everrrrrr," says Agnes in her booger voice. "I promise."

CHAPTER TWO

NOW IT IS THE MORNING of the first day of school and Mrs. Parker is holding up a sack lunch. "I drew a little heart here by your name," she says, smiling. "Is that too embarrassing?"

"Yes," says Agnes. "But I understand that you have to do these mom things."

Mrs. Parker gives her head a little shake and drops a bag full of grapes in the sack. "I can't believe it's already your last year of elementary school!" she says.

"Me neither," says Agnes. She pours herself a bowl of raisin bran and says another little prayer that she and Prejean will be in the same class. She also prays again that she will not, please God, get stuck with Mrs.

Libonati. Why can't Neidermeyer get Libbo? And why do these brand-new shoes feel so uncomfortable already? And what if all the girls in the whole class except Agnes show up wearing bras?

"Mom," she says. "Did you wear a bra in sixth grade?"

Mrs. Parker, who has been banging cupboard doors open and shut, becomes still. She turns to face Agnes. "No. I wanted to, but my mother said I wasn't ready." Then she lowers her head and looks deep into Agnes's eyes. "Agnes, do you want a bra?"

"Good morning!" says Mr. Parker.

Agnes widens her eyes, sending an urgent psychic message to her mother. *Ix-nay on the a-bray!!*

Mrs. Parker simply picks up the sack lunch, puts it into Agnes's hands, and says, "Big day today!"

Mr. Parker looks puzzled. "It is?" he says.

Agnes holds up her lunch.

"Boy," says Mr. Parker, shaking his head. "I need coffee." He kisses Agnes on the head and pours himself a cup. "Hard to believe you're twelve already," he says.

"That's because I'm *eleven*, Dad," says Agnes. "Till February." Agnes's father is a dreamy type who likes to spend a lot of time in his head. Her mother calls him "tall, dark, and absentminded."

Mr. Parker says, "Mmm." He stares out the window, sipping coffee. Mrs. Parker sighs. Agnes leans back in her chair, going through her checklist of things to worry about.

At school Agnes and Prejean jostle with a crowd of other kids in front of the big bulletin board in the breezeway. Agnes is squinting to focus but can't read a thing. *How weird.* It wasn't this bad last year. She tries to force her way closer to the board but stops when Prejean says, "Rats! You got Libbo." Agnes slumps. "So did Neidermeyer." Agnes gasps. "But so did I!" Prejean raises her palm. Agnes slaps it, loving the sting.

Mrs. Libonati favors patent-leather pumps with gold buckles, big plaid jackets with jeweled buttons, and tremendous shoulder pads. She gives you the impression that bumping into her would really hurt. She is what the sixth graders call a *hard case.* And it just seems so true. There is something *hard* about her. Her hair, for one thing. It does not move, ever. It is well known that she keeps two full-size cans of Final Net in her desk drawer.

Agnes's baby-sitter, who was one of Libbo's students, told Agnes and Prejean all kinds of things. Such as, Libbo will not touch chalk with her bare hands because she believes it dries out her skin. To get around this she uses a long, black, shiny chalk holder that makes her look like an old movie actress holding a cigarette. She walks around the classroom in a rigid scissor-step, swinging one patent-leather pump in front of the other. Also, she will flunk you for practically anything. No name on your paper? *F!* Written in pencil? *F!*

Mrs. Libonati opens her classroom door. All the students are silent, but she still looks aggravated. She folds and refolds her arms. "I want you lined up in *alphabetical order,* people!" she commands. "By last name. You do know your alphabet by now, don't you?"

Prejean waves to Agnes and walks off to find a spot near the front of the line. The kids are bumping shoulders and giggling. Agnes steps into her slot behind Jay Metzger, when, *ouch,* somebody elbows her in the ribs.

"*N* before *P,*" growls Neidermeyer.

Agnes stands with her mouth open. "Uhhh . . ."

"Didn't ask you to *open wide.* Asked you to *step aside.*"

Agnes moves two steps back and lets her in.

"So, Gagness, didja have a nice quiet summer? Build a lot of things outta Popsicle sticks? Oh, and how's the sock collection coming?" Neidermeyer rubs her hands together. "Ooooo," she squeals, "*sounds fun!*"

"Face the front, people! No talking," barks Libbo.

Agnes simmers. As she thinks of how easy it would be to pull Neidermeyer's stupid scraggly ponytail, Brian Olansky scoots in between them.

"File in!" trumpets Mrs. Libonati.

In the classroom every desk already has a name on

it. Agnes is happy to find herself seated at the back of a row. The farther from Libbo the better.

"As I get to know you," says Libbo, scissor-stepping among her new recruits, "I will find out who your little buddies are. I *will* separate you. Because you *will* pay attention in this class. And you *will not* talk to your neighbor. And if you do talk to your neighbor, you *will* spend the rest of the period in the hallway. Standing. Without a book, without a chair . . ."

Without a prayer, thinks Agnes. She wants to roll her eyes but does not.

"Now, you may think," says Libbo with her first hint of a smile, "that since this is the first day of school, this is a goof-off day. Am I right?" She pauses and nods, grinning, assuming agreement with the whole class. Suddenly the smile collapses. "It is *not*!" she says. "Today you will start working on your first report! You will now be Native Americans.

"*You,*" she says, pointing a perfectly lacquered nail at Stephen Arnett, "are Tecumseh. *You,*" she says, continuing to Ashley Cardell, "are Pocahontas."

Ashley smiles, finding herself ever so adorable. *Yecch!* thinks Agnes. Ashley is famous for telling everyone how her mother forbids her to share her hairbrush at school. *Lice,* you know . . .

"*You,*" continues Libbo, pointing at Triana Dawes, "are Sacajawea. And I hope you people are writing this down, because I am not—repeat, am *not*—going to say this twice. . . ."

Agnes is way down the row. Libbo has run out of girl Native Americans. She watches as Prejean is named "Sequoia." Finally, she is one seat away, naming Brian Olansky "Sitting Bull." Agnes's palms are so sweaty, her pencil is squishing around in her hands—all because she is about to be pointed at by Mrs. Libonati.

"*You,*" says Mrs. Libonati, locking her burning eyes on Agnes, "are . . ." And here she pauses. She pinches the bridge of her nose. She wags her finger back and forth while trying to recover her memory. Agnes hypnotically follows the finger. "You are . . . *Squanto!*" Agnes jumps in her seat. The rest of the class bursts into hoots and cackling.

"*Students!*" shouts Libbo. "Did I say something *funny? Did I?*" She paces. "Do some of you, by chance, want to spend your very first morning in school copying the dictionary?" She places her hands on her hips and surveys the room. She says the word "*Squanto!*"—and looks around quickly, eagle-eyed.

Silence. Libbo turns her back and marches toward her desk. Suddenly, she spins on her heel—"*Squanto!*" she hisses fiercely.

Someone lets loose with a tremendous snort. Mrs. Libonati's nostrils flare. "*You! Out! Hallway!*"

All eyes turn to the offender. *Neidermeyer!* She stands

up and then walks slowly and deliberately, like a prisoner of war. It is obvious that she is itching to slam the door on her way out, but even Neidermeyer is cowed by Mrs. Libonati. As she passes, she shoots Agnes a look of smoldering fury. "But I didn't do anything!" Agnes wants to cry.

At lunch she learns that Neidermeyer has convinced Brian and his friends to take turns sneaking up behind Agnes and whispering *"Squanto!"* in her ear. *Oh, rats.* And it's only the first day.

Agnes stares into space and listens to Ashley Cardell telling Natalie Kim all about her costume for Pocahontas. "Okay. So. It's sort of like the movie, you know? Because, like, I already have this perfect dress that's like off the shoulder? And my mom? She has, like, these moccasins with turquoise that she got from New Mexico? And they are real leather . . . ?"

Wait a minute. Agnes is stunned. "Hey, Ashley," she says. "You're going to be wearing some kind of costume?"

"Of course," says Ashley, with a showy touch of exasperation, "you're *supposed* to."

"Didn't you know?" Prejean asks Agnes. "It's a Libbo thing. You have to *be* the person. You have to dress up like them and pretend you are them and give a speech and everything."

Agnes cannot imagine what kind of clothing Squanto

wears but is pretty sure it is nothing off the shoulder. She will have to give a speech standing in front of the entire class. In Squanto clothes. She pictures herself saying, "Hello. I'm *Squanto*!" This thing will just go *on* and *on* and *on* . . .

Back in class for math, Agnes figures that she must be extra-nervous or coming down with something, because she cannot focus on the board. Mrs. Libonati is drawing a number line. Agnes can see the big zero in the middle, but not much else. She finds that if she stretches the skin at the corners of her eyes, the board becomes readable again. It is a tiring thing to do, but it works.

Mrs. Libonati is in the midst of adding negative five to positive one when she stops abruptly and points. At *Agnes*. "You. Yes, with the fingers in your eyes. What in the *world* are you doing?"

"I, um, can't see," says Agnes.

"Stand up," commands Libbo. She walks to the back of the class and drags Agnes's desk to the front. Agnes follows like a sheep as the desk rasps against the floor. Libbo parks the desk smack dab in front of the board. "That better?" she asks. Agnes nods. "All right, then!"

At the end of the day—which somehow takes forty-six hours to get to—Mrs. Libonati calls to Agnes. "Miss . . . Parker, is it?" she says. "Please take this note home to your parents." Agnes reaches for the blue slip and is surprised when Libbo takes her hand and *pats* it. She is holding hands with Mrs. Libonati! "You need glasses, my dear," says Mrs. L. "When you are able to see properly, I will return you to alphabetical order."

Agnes wanders numbly out the door and meets Prejean waiting for her in the breezeway. "Libbo says I need glasses."

"Cool!" says Prejean.

Cool? Agnes Parker has the best best friend ever.

That Friday after school, Mrs. Parker is seated in the optometrist's waiting room when Agnes stumbles in wearing too-big, disposable sunglasses. With her pupils dilated, everything appears to her as if it is floating in fog. The doctor has diagnosed Agnes as nearsighted and has urged her to select some frames right away. Her mother leads her by the hand down the hall to a room filled with eyeglasses of every kind and shape.

"My gosh," says Agnes, squinting into a mirror. "How am I supposed to pick anything out?"

"I'll help," says Mrs. Parker, pulling a few selections from a rack of wire frames. When she turns around and sidles up to Agnes, she is wearing baby-blue cat-eye spectacles encrusted at the corners with rhinestones. "Now, you *can't* have these, sweetie. These are mine. Ah, gla-moor!"

"Mom, please," Agnes whispers.

"Okay, honey," says Mrs. Parker. She removes Agnes's cardboard sunglasses and slips a pair of wire frames over her face. "What do you think?"

These glasses are almost invisible—how wonderful! She tries on a few others: one with a touch of tortoise-shell at the arms, one twinkly golden pair, another, a dark pewter that makes her look like a scientist—and always returns to her mother's very first choice. Agnes leans so close to the mirror that she clouds it with her breath. "I like these," she says.

"They're the ones I'd pick," says Mrs. Parker. "You know? I think they make you look pretty . . . in a grown-up sort of way."

Settled. And they can be ready today! It is a silly thing, and Agnes knows it, but she has always thought that people with glasses seemed mysterious. Perhaps this is because her father wears them and takes them off only to sleep or shower. He is always squinty with-out them; and his eyelids look strangely pale.

On the way home Mrs. Parker stops at the main library on Harvard Street. Agnes must check out special books for her American Indian report. Mrs. Parker helps practically blind Agnes to sort through the shelves for books on Squanto. "Bingo!" she says. "Here, can you see his picture on the cover?"

"Yes," says Agnes. It is an old pea-green book with black pen illustrations. One shows Squanto bending over a stalk of corn. He is shirtless and wearing nothing but little squares of leather in front and behind. He is practically naked. She turns the pages quickly, her nose three inches from the page. *Ugh. This book even smells old and moldy.* In every single picture Squanto is all skin!

"Hey!" says Mrs. Parker. "This one looks good!" She hands her a glossy book with a richly detailed oil painting of Squanto on the cover. He is holding a stalk of corn looking calm and in control. And he is wrapped in an absolutely beautiful blanket. *I can do that!* thinks Agnes.

Mrs. Parker and Agnes sit down on the carpeted floor together. "From what I can remember," says Mrs. Parker, "Squanto was famous for his fish fertilizer." She picks up the old stinky book and locates a picture of Squanto placing dead fish at the root of a cornstalk.

Agnes pictures herself in front of the class, wrapped in a blanket, holding a basket of paper fish. *Hey, the fish could be pretty!* Two-sided rainbow trout, stuffed with cotton balls in the middle to make them look three-dimensional . . . A cinch. She already has the heavy ivory artist's paper, the watercolors. If she could just get her eyesight back, she would start working on them the minute she got home. Agnes loves projects. This could be okay.

Chapter Three

Agnes has all weekend to get used to her new glasses. They are not quite as invisible as she first thought. But the things she can see now! The old sycamore across the street has hundreds and hundreds of distinctly multi-pointed leaves. She can read the kitchen clock from the dining room, all the titles in the bookcase, and the settings on the VCR. And in the larger world, street signs and the license plates of passing cars are crystal clear.

At the grocery store Agnes can't get over how crisp and complicated each label is on every can of soup. Is this what everyone else sees? And when she and her mother are standing in line at the cash register, Agnes sees . . . a boy.

He is standing in front of her in line along with his father. He is bending over a roll of candy—SweeTarts—and unwrapping the foil from the top. Agnes takes in his every detail: the brown skin at the back of his neck, the glossy-black, near-perfect clipped hair, the wonderfully scrubbed and shiny ears. And then she catches a glimpse of his profile: dark brown eyes with thick, straight lashes, a nose that is precisely shaped, almost sharp.

He flicks a SweeTart into the air and catches it, with grace, in his open mouth. Agnes watches his jaws move; he even has an interesting way of chewing! He flicks another piece of candy, but this one goes wide. He backs up to catch it and stomps on Agnes's foot. He turns around, surprised, and lifts his fascinating eyebrows. He is about to speak, when his father takes over.

"Joe, please!" He takes away the candy and turns to Agnes and her mother. "Please pardon us."

"No problem," says Mrs. Parker. Joe and Agnes are locked in a stare until Agnes suddenly pretends to become absorbed in the display of sugarless gum. When Joe turns back around, however, she continues to sneak peeks at his neck and ears and eyelashes. What is it about him? He seems to be ultra three-dimensional. Or is he just *exceptionally clean* for a boy? When he and his father finally go, she is somehow relieved—although she can't keep her eyes off him until he is out the door.

Agnes takes off her glasses and the store dissolves into a blur. She puts them on again: Everything regains its crispness. *Wow. Must be the glasses.*

At school on Monday morning Prejean sticks close to Agnes. It seems that every sixth grader they pass says, "Hey! You got glasses!" To which Agnes replies, "I know!"

"Agnes," says Prejean, "if I ever get glasses, I am going to get some just like those. They are cool-looking, plus they are almost invisible!"

Agnes doubts that Prejean will ever need glasses. To her, Prejean is practically a perfect person. (Although she can be stubborn as a mule.) And not only does she have perfect eyesight, she can always see trouble coming way before Agnes even has a clue.

"Uh-oh, jerk alert," says Prejean. Down the hall, Neidermeyer and her redheaded sidekick, Carmella Shade, saunter their way. Neidermeyer has obviously trained her sights on Agnes. When she passes, she squinches up her eye and sneers.

"Yo, Professor Geeky," she says. "How's them four eyes?" Carmella gives her buddy a congratulatory chuckle.

"Fun-ny. Four eyes. Never heard *that* one before," says Prejean. "No wonder Carmella finds it soooo hysterical."

Neidermeyer clicks her heels and gives a sharp

salute. "The better to see you with, my dear!" she bellows, while Carmella practically collapses with laughter.

Prejean turns to Agnes. "Oh; my. Just *too* entertaining. Let's go, shall we?"

Agnes is glad to return to her old desk at the back of the room. Being able to look at everybody else without being looked at so much herself makes her feel peaceful—like she does when she sits on the roof.

At home Agnes's bedroom has a dormer window where she likes to perch with her legs hanging over the edge. She has to climb on her old chest of drawers to get up there, but it is worth it. There is no better place to read. And it is the absolute best place to eat sunflower seeds and spit the shells down on the lawn. Sometimes Mrs. Waldrip, the Parkers' neighbor, will venture out into her backyard. Agnes loves to sit extra still and watch her hang her laundry or work in her garden. Why is it that everyone seems more interesting when viewed from afar?

Agnes sees something out of the corner of her eye and feels a soft *poink* in her hair above her ear. Paper airplane. She opens it. "Where's Libbo?" it says, in Prejean's handwriting. Mrs. Libonati is almost ten minutes late.

Back in the corner of the class, one of the boys makes a noise—"*Thbbbbbbbbbbbbbttt!*"—sounding just like the air escaping from a spit-filled balloon. Brian Olansky echoes back, "*Thbbbbbbbbbbbbbttttt!*" Soon the classroom is alive with these sounds. Ashley Cardell claps her hands over her ears. "Shut up!" she says.

Brian chucks a wadded-up paper ball at Ashley. "Shut up!" he whines in what he thinks is a girly voice. Agnes sighs. There are definite drawbacks to sitting behind Brian.

Ashley picks up the paper wad and throws it back. Brian returns the favor by sending along two more. Ashley, looking like an angry kitten, hurls her pencil at Brian. But she releases the pencil too soon, and it flies straight up in the air until—*thunk*—it sticks in the soft ceiling tile right above Brian's head. Brian says, "Wow!" Soon he has five friends crowding around his desk gazing at the stuck pencil, and Agnes is feeling claustrophobic.

Brian tries a pencil of his own. *Thwack!* It goes up like a rocket and sticks perfectly. "Cool!" Brian's friend Jay doesn't have the same luck. His pencil hits the ceiling and bounces off. "It has to be sharp, stupid," says Brian.

Now almost the entire class has gathered under this spot of ceiling. The pencil sharpener is grinding away as kids stand in line to hone their tiny spears. Agnes is surrounded by jostling bodies. Somewhere in the mob she can hear Prejean's voice but can't see where she is.

"*Class!*"

Everyone freezes. Agnes cannot see Mrs. Libonati but

looks up through the crowd at the ceiling. There must be at least fifteen pencils stuck there. A few of the kids try to slink off to their desks.

"*Those* of you who are out of your seats, *remain* standing," Mrs. Libonati announces. "I want each and every one of you in line at the board." The herd surges forward. *"Wait!"* says Mrs. Libonati. "Proceed to the board in an orderly fashion. And when you get to the board, write down your name and be seated. Those people whose names are on my board will *not* be attending first recess this morning."

There is a collective groan. Unfortunately, Prejean is among the caught. Agnes rests her chin in her hands and breathes deeply as the surrounding crowd of students departs. She looks over at Mrs. Libonati and sees . . . ohmigosh . . . standing right there beside her . . . SweeTart boy!

"Boys and girls," says Libbo, resting her hand on the boy's shoulder, "we have a new student with us today. His name is Joe Waldrip."

Waldrip? Waldrip! Like old-timey Mrs. Waldrip? Who hangs her wash out on the line and wears a hairnet over her curlers? Agnes can feel herself flushing. It is as if the air around her head were suddenly getting tighter. She prays no one notices.

"I regret, Joe, that you have not seen our class on its best behavior this morning."

Joe just smiles and shrugs.

"You will be interested to know," continues Mrs. Libonati, "that Joe is an actual descendant of Chief Joseph of the Nez Perce tribe, on his mother's side. And so he will be reporting on his ancestor when we do our Native American reports in four weeks."

Neidermeyer raises her hand. "You know what is so weird, Mrs. L.? I just found out that my great-great-great-great-great-grandfather came over on the *Mayflower*." Neidermeyer sparkles with pride and looks directly at Joe. The self-congratulating expression on Neidermeyer's face makes Agnes queasy. Joe just shrugs and smiles again.

When the first recess bell rings, only about a quarter of the class is allowed to stand up and leave. Agnes is busting to talk to Prejean about Joe. What a day to be stranded at recess by herself.

Surprisingly, Neidermeyer is also out on the playground. She must have gotten back to her seat just before Libonati came in. Carmella Shade is being held back in class, and there aren't enough sixth-grade kids to get a softball game started, so even Neidermeyer is wandering around looking uncharacteristically lost.

Agnes moves her eyes around without moving her head, trying to casually catch sight of Joe. She tells herself she just wants to get a look at him, that's *all*.

"Hey. Weren't you at the grocery store yesterday?"

Joe's voice is raspy and warm. He sounds like someone with a sore throat. But still, it's a nice voice.

Agnes wheels around. "Yes." She notices she sounds a bit choked.

"I thought that was you." He smiles.

What a wonderful face he has with that smile and those chocolate-colored eyes. Everything about him is a hundred percent friendly. And he is talking to her!

"So," says Agnes with a gulp, "do you know the Waldrips?" Never has her voice sounded so high-pitched. "We have Waldrips in our neighborhood."

"Yeah. That's my grandmother," says Joe.

"Oh!" says Agnes. "She lives right behind me. I mean, right across the fence—"

"Hey, *I* live right behind you. Me and my dad and my brother," he says to Agnes. "We're staying there for a while. But we're looking for our own house."

Agnes would love to take this nugget of information away with her and think about it in private. She knows that if she stands there much longer with her mouth hanging open, Joe will think she's a zombie. Suddenly, a distraction arrives. Circling them, walking on her *hands* of all things, is Neidermeyer.

"Yo. What's up?" she asks. Then she flips back and lands on her feet. "So, you play ball?" she asks Joe. Neidermeyer is just so . . . *herself*. And, of course, she pretends that Agnes is invisible.

Joe reveals that he does indeed play ball. Basketball. Soccer. Baseball. And he was a Little League All-Star. "No way!" says Neidermeyer. "I'm an All-Star, too. Last three years."

"On a girls' team?" Joe asks.

"Yeah, so what?" says Neidermeyer. "I'm still the best player in school, period. Ask any guy here."

They start talking about things like pitching speed and division championships. Which then leads to the topics of professional sports, home-run averages, and their mutual worship of the Chicago Cubs.

Agnes will play an occasional game of kick ball or softball at recess but is not much interested otherwise. Her father is even more like this. He wouldn't have any idea which channel to punch for ESPN.

For at least six minutes, Agnes stands mute and awkward. She certainly can't add to Joe's and Neidermeyer's inexhaustible facts and opinions about this year's World Series play-offs—but she doesn't want to just slink off. After all, Joe *was* talking to her first. What to say, what to say?

"I think we might just have to write off our chances until next year's draft," says Joe.

"No kidding," agrees Neidermeyer. "And the pitching has been miserable. *Really* blows."

Agnes briefly imagines herself talking to Joe like that, one hand on her hip and her eye squinched up.

"*Really* blows . . ." Maybe the next time she sees him, she can just do a back flip. "Yo!" she will say. Standing there, she goes through her mental catalog of Neider-meyer mannerisms. That bored sprawl she does when confined to her desk where her legs stick out in the aisle . . . That toss of her head and the scornful "Tch!" sound she makes whenever she thinks anyone has said something stupid . . .

The bell sounds, and Joe and Neidermeyer are still trading sports stories, walking together while Agnes lags behind. Every once in a while, Neidermeyer glances over her shoulder and shoots Agnes an ugly cross-eyed look—her rendition of Agnes in glasses.

Oh, to be more talky, more grabby, more brave. More hugely well informed of the comings and goings of the Chicago Cubs. If only Prejean were here . . .

Man, Agnes says to herself, *why am I always the one walking around feeling squished by her?*

Back in class, all the punished students have been working on an essay called "My Most Memorable Moment." Agnes knows that the minute a teacher asks you to write about stuff like this, every memorable moment disappears. So you invent something very, very lame.

Libbo is collecting the essays when something stops her square in front of Pat Marie Hinkle's desk. Actually, she is mostly called Fat Marie, a nickname stuck to her years ago. Pat Marie is alone a lot. She used to have a quiet, skinny, almost ghostly-looking friend named Lee Ann Greenglass who moved last spring. So far, Pat Marie has not found a replacement for her.

"Pat Marie, this essay is only one sentence long," says Mrs. Libonati.

"Mm-hm," says Pat Marie, focusing her eyes on the top of her desk.

"'My Most Memorable Moment,'" reads Libbo. "'The time they let me back into McDonald's.'" Mrs. Libonati drops her hands to her sides. "'The *end*'?"

Pat Marie does not reply.

"I think you need to add some more detail, don't you?"

Pat Marie nods silently.

"Bring this back to me tomorrow. And tell the whole story this time. You can read it to us in the morning."

Agnes knows this means that Pat Marie is going to have a terrible day. And a terrible tomorrow. She sees Neidermeyer whispering in Carmella's ear. Then Carmella signals to Brian, whose shoulders are already shaking with his nasty chuckling. Pat Marie's ears are sticking out through her straight hair and they are fiery red. Agnes knows that exact feeling.

At least Agnes always has Prejean. But who does Pat Marie have? Just Neidermeyer and Carmella and loud-mouthed boys like Brian Olansky on her case. Agnes knows that without Prejean, she really is *just inches* from being another Pat Marie. *Ugh.*

Agnes wants to stand between Pat Marie and Neidermeyer like a shield. It is not easy to picture.

But as Neidermeyer smirks, Agnes folds her arms and comes to a quiet decision.

We'll see, Neidermeyer, she says to herself. *We'll see . . .*

CHAPTER FOUR

Dear Mrs. Libonati,

I am not going to tell you who I am because it is not important. I just thought you should know something about Pat Marie. Everyone makes fun of her for being fat. I think that she will get teased if you make her read her paper about McDonald's today. Maybe you could just talk to her about it in private instead. I hope this does not make you mad . . .

Agnes erases that last line. *Of course* this letter is going to make Mrs. Libonati mad! That is what makes it so nerve-racking to write, and even scarier to deliver. She had a hard time getting to sleep last night just thinking about it.

She signs the letter *from a student,* folds it, and sticks it into an envelope that is decorated with daisies. The daisies don't look forceful enough, but this is the only stationery she owns. She writes *Mrs. Libonati* on the front and sticks the letter into her backpack.

In the kitchen Mr. Parker is at his customary place by the window, sipping coffee and staring. Agnes has no idea what it is he dreams about there every morning. He asks her, "How's school?" but doesn't turn his head.

"Fine," says Agnes. And then she adds, "Except for the usual jerks."

"You mean bullies?" he asks.

Agnes is a little shocked to have her father's full attention. "Just some mean kids at school," she says.

"Are they hitting people?" asks Mr. Parker.

"Umm, no."

"What do they do?" Mr. Parker pulls up a chair.

"Oh, you know. They call people fat or gay and make fun of them. . . ."

"Some things never change," says Mr. Parker.

Agnes looks at her father's face. That his eyes look extra big behind his glasses gives her a funny pang. She pictures Neidermeyer bellowing, *What big eyes you have!* "Did you get teased a lot?" she asks.

"Me?" says Mr. Parker as if the question has caught him off guard. "Not really."

Agnes watches her father crane his neck and look around. He lowers his voice. "It was your mother."

What? Agnes knows her mother as the most unafraid, friendly person she has ever seen. They cannot go out for pizza without her making friends with the teenage waiter. Dorothy, the mean ball-stealing eighty-five-year-old lady across the street, thinks of Mrs. Parker as her own daughter, and brings her beautiful floppy bunches of roses from her garden.

"It was pretty awful," whispers Mr. Parker.

"Agnes!" calls Mrs. Parker from the entryway. "If you want a ride, you'd better be ready now!"

Poor Mom, thinks Agnes.

"Agnes!" Mrs. Parker yells again.

Agnes is careful not to ask her mother anything specific during the ride to school. "Mom?" she says. "What do you think about people who make fun of people?"

"Is someone making fun of you?" Mrs. Parker quickly asks.

"No. I'm just talking about kids who make fun of other kids. Just generally."

Mrs. Parker stops at a light. She turns to Agnes and looks her straight in the eyes. "If someone makes fun of you, I am giving you permission to pinch them. You can pinch them as hard as you want. Do you understand?"

"Oh, Mom, no one's making fun of me," says Agnes. "Really."

"*Pinch* them," says Mrs. Parker emphatically.

"Okay," says Agnes.

"And if that gets you in trouble, have them call me from the office." After a few moments of silence she mutters, "So help me God . . ."

All her life Agnes has heard her mother talking about how violence never solves anything; how important it is to "use your words." But she knows she is not kidding about the pinching.

When they pull up at the school, her mother grabs her face and gives her a hard kiss on the cheek. "I love you, Agnes," she says. Her eyes are bright and she gives her head a sharp nod. It is exactly the expression she wore the first time Agnes jumped off the high dive at Sandy Lake.

Agnes nods back, slams the car door, and runs to classroom 5. It is empty and unlocked and vaguely spooky. There is a half cup of coffee with a huge lipstick smudge and a heavy key chain with gold bangles sitting on Mrs. Libonati's desk. Agnes, almost dizzy with fright, places her envelope in the center of the desk, picks up the keys, and plunks them down on top as a sort of paperweight. Wishing she could just vaporize, she slowly cracks open the door, slips out sideways— and is free!

Prejean is sitting on a bench around the corner. "Where have you been?" she asks.

"My mom took me this morning," says Agnes, still feeling flushed and light-headed. She has *never* kept a secret from her best friend. But at the same time, somewhere in her heart, Agnes feels that telling *anyone* about the note would change her reason for leaving it. That would turn it into a show-offy thing. And that would leave her feeling a little—not right, and kind of ashamed.

In class Mrs. Libonati gives no clue of having read the letter, even though it is now missing from her desk. And as the day moves into noon, she still doesn't ask Pat Marie to read her essay. At lunch Agnes eyes Pat Marie alone at the end of the cafeteria table. She thinks of herself as her secret friend. Should she sit down by her, ask her how she's doing?

"Looks like Neidermeyer has a new best buddy," says Prejean, pointing with her sandwich.

Joe and Neidermeyer are having lunch together. Carmella is shoved to the side and is straining to keep up with the conversation between the two.

Last night Agnes spent a whole hour perched on top of her dresser, staring out at the Waldrips' backyard. Once in a while her heart would receive a little shock when Mrs. Waldrip showed up at the kitchen window. But other than that, there were only the blue shadows of the television moving behind the drapes in the den.

And today, whenever she catches a glimpse of him,

there is a light that shines around him and separates him from the rest of the crowd. *Just look at him.* Even Neidermeyer, who usually mows everyone down like a steamroller, has stopped and singled out Joe. Even she can't miss that light.

"Agnes, I'm *over here,*" says Prejean.

"I know," says Agnes.

"But you're looking *over there.* And I'm talking and talking and you're not listening."

"And now you're mad at me?" says Agnes.

"Aren't I supposed to be?" says Prejean.

"I'm sorry," says Agnes. She picks up her little package of Oreos, Prejean's favorite. "For you, my tiny flower," she says.

Prejean sighs and hands Agnes a little bag full of barbecue potato chips. The ruffled kind. A peace offering. "For you, my dahling . . ."

Now it is the last class of the day, language arts. Lately, Mrs. Libonati has been allowing her students to use the free reading time in order to prepare for their American Indian reports. Today, however, Libbo says she has something to read aloud, herself.

"'My Most Memorable Moment, by Pat Marie Hinkle,'" reads Mrs. Libonati. "'The time they let me back into McDonald's.'"

Immediately, half the class starts tittering. Agnes feels hot. So, Libbo just could not keep it to herself.

That Libbo! Such a hard case! Agnes sees Pat Marie sitting with her neck buried in her shoulders, as if she wishes she could pull her head in like a turtle.

"'This moment is special to me,'" reads Mrs. Libonati, "'because it was the night before my best friend moved to Chicago. Her name is Lee Ann. She was scared to move because she lived here her whole life. And the day before she moved, she lost her ballerina charm. This made her even more afraid because it was something from her grandma who died. So everything felt like bad luck.

"'Lee Ann was crying. We looked everywhere for her charm and it was terrible. I went to bed that night and kept on thinking about it. Then I closed my eyes and saw McDonald's. My mom stopped there for coffee that morning when she took us to school. I ran downstairs and told my mom and dad I had to go back because I just knew the charm was there. They let me put my coat on over my pajamas and took me there. At first I thought it was in the bathroom, but I couldn't find it. Then I found out someone had picked it up in the bathroom and gave it to the people at the cash register. I got the charm. And I gave it back to Lee Ann at the airport. The end.'"

Mrs. Libonati looks up from the paper. Agnes has noticed that Libbo has a certain crocodile smile she uses when she is about to come down hard on a kid. It is a thin-lipped smile that shows way too many teeth. But this particular smile doesn't have even a hint of crocodile in it. "Compare this to yesterday's paper. This essay tells us so many things," says Mrs. Libonati. She walks to the board and picks up her black enameled chalk holder. She writes in bold letters: *Pat Marie.* "Because Pat Marie told us her story in detail, we learned some important things about her. Who can name something they learned?"

The class seems momentarily shy. Agnes wants to but is too frozen to raise her hand. "I learned that Pat Marie is loyal," Natalie finally says.

Loyal, writes Mrs. Libonati. "Anyone else?"

Ashley raises a hand. "Um, I learned that she has, like, a good memory?"

Good memory, writes Mrs. Libonati, nodding her head in agreement.

Brian waves his hand in a funny way. He bends his elbow and holds his arm scrunched up next to his body. He sort of twinkles his fingers.

"Brian?" says Mrs. Libonati.

Brian looks quickly over at Neidermeyer, then assumes a deadpan gaze—something he always does when he thinks he is about to be hilarious. "I learned that Pat Marie loves to eat at McDonald's," he says.

Mrs. Libonati wears an expression every bit as blank as Brian's. She stands completely still and holds his gaze.

"And how did you learn that?" says Mrs. Libonati at last.

"She says so," says Brian.

"Where?" says Mrs. Libonati.

"On that paper . . ." Brian's voice is a bit quieter now.

"Hmmmm. Let's see." Mrs. Libonati picks up Pat Marie's "Most Memorable Moment" and squints. She even turns the page over to the blank side and looks there. "No, Brian. All I see here is that Pat Marie's mother likes to stop there for coffee."

Brian says, "Oh."

"I don't think you were paying attention," says Mrs. L. "Were you, Brian?"

Brian is silent.

"I want you to come up with something else," says Mrs. Libonati, smiling—this time *with tons* of crocodile.

Brian swallows. "I think . . . that . . . uh . . . Pat Marie is . . ."

"Yes?"

"I think that Pat Marie is a good friend." He says it quickly and lets out a deep sigh.

"Very good!" agrees Mrs. Libonati. "Her essay showed this very well."

From this point on, everyone in the class comes up with praise for Pat Marie. *Concerned. Helpful. Sensitive. Brave. Loving.* Someone even suggests *Heroic,* but Mrs. Libonati does not write that one down.

"I think this about does it," says Mrs. Libonati. "But before we all go home, I want to have a turn, too. Do you know what I learned about you, Pat Marie?"

By this time, Pat Marie wears the dazed look of someone who just had a suitcase dropped on her head.

"I learned," continues her teacher, "that you are a very special girl. Because it is not everybody who can take another person's feelings as seriously as they do their own. That is the ingredient needed to be a good friend—and a good person." Then, in her clipped and businesslike manner she says, "Class dismissed."

Agnes continues to sit in her chair. She watches as Mrs. Libonati strides toward her desk with that perfect posture. *Smack. Smack.* She gathers each stack of papers and squares them up on her desk before tucking them into her big leather portfolio. She reminds Agnes of a soldier—one who fights for the good guys. Agnes sends her a silent message. *Thank you, thank you, Mrs. Libonati.*

"You know," says Prejean on the walk home from school, "Libbo is different from what they said."

"I think the sixth graders just like to scare everybody," says Agnes. Prejean agrees.

Agnes and Prejean take their customary walk through the "shortcut woods," a green, leafy place not yet mowed down for new houses. The autumn light shines through the trees at a slant, its beams filled with golden dust. Agnes loves the mellow sunshine and air that tastes like menthol cough drops. "I almost forget how much I love fall," says Agnes. "Maybe because I never want summer vacation to end." She stretches out her arms, wishing she could gather up all the coils of blackberry bushes, the incense-fragrant pines, and the crunchy sycamores in a big great-smelling bouquet.

"I love the fall!!" someone shrieks from behind.

Agnes and Prejean turn to see Neidermeyer with her hands clutched to her heart. She is walking with Joe Waldrip. "Everything is so *bee-yoo-tee-ful*!" exclaims Neidermeyer, throwing her hands in the air. She waltzes about a bit, staggering. Finally, she hugs a tree.

"Oh, yeah?" says Prejean. "Well, I *adore* the fall because everything is so *fab-u-lous*!" She gives a glamorous wave to an imaginary crowd, the one beauty queens do that makes them look as if they are lovingly polishing a windshield.

"I *salivate* over fall because it is so *splen-dif-forus*!" Agnes calls out, surprising herself. She snaps her fingers like a flamenco dancer and grabs Prejean's hand. Together they turn and skip through the forest singing, "Tra-la-la fall! La-di-dah fall! Do-re-mi fall!"

And as she skips away, Agnes hears someone laughing. Joe!

At home Agnes throws down her backpack, kicks off her shoes, and skids into the kitchen. Mrs. Parker is sitting there with a cup of tea, a calculator, and a pile of paper. She looks up at her daughter and says, rather carefully, "So, anybody get pinched today?"

Agnes throws her arms around her mother's neck. "I didn't have to pinch a single person," says Agnes. *But if I had to, I would have. And I would have done it for you,* she thinks to herself.

Mrs. Parker grabs one of Agnes's hands and kisses it. "Good girl," she says. "Good girl."

"Good mom," says Agnes, returning the kiss. "Good mom."

CHAPTER FIVE

AGNES AND PREJEAN are having their regular Saturday morning phone call. Usually they talk about Tiff and Zori and what happened that morning on Planet Z. And Agnes *does* mean to get to that. But right now she's noticed that there's smoke coming out of the chimney at Joe's house, and that gets her wondering: How long has he been up? What does Prejean think he does on weekends? Does she think Neidermeyer will be coming over?

"Agnes, I'm not bored," Prejean suddenly declares. "I *swear* I'm not. I could talk about Joe *all morning*!"

Agnes is startled. "Do you really think I'm talking about him too much?"

"Of course not," says Prejean. "And there's still so much more to cover. We haven't discussed his possible favorite sandwich or what side he parts his hair on—"

"He doesn't wear a part," says Agnes. "He combs his hair straight up."

"Ooooo. Just a minute! Let me write that down!"

Prejean is trying to be funny, but Agnes would rather not be teased about this. "I just thought you'd want to know about him, that's all," says Agnes. "I mean, he's new and I'm not saying that I *know* him, but I thought . . ."

Prejean interrupts with a loud yawn. "So, are we going to ride bikes, or what? Can you break away from watching Joe's chimney long enough to make time for your old, boring, faithful friend?"

"Okay, okay, at eleven-thirty," says Agnes, smarting a little. "I'm going to work on my Squanto thing first."

"Remember," says Prejean, "eleven-thirty means eleven-thirty! Write it down on your hand if you have to."

"Right," says Agnes. But she doesn't. Agnes knows Prejean hates to be kept waiting, and she plans to be on time.

Since it is a particularly beautiful Saturday morning and the air is still, Agnes decides to take her paints to the back patio. She has already spent a lot of time painstakingly sketching life-size fish, copying them out of the encyclopedia. Now she has to give them color, cut them out, glue them together, and stuff them.

As Agnes cuts paper, she thinks about Squanto. How he went to England, came back to America, and was captured by Spaniards. How in Spain he was sold as a slave. And then he went back to North America, only to find his whole tribe had been wiped out by a plague. And finally he ended up being most famous for helping the Pilgrims at Plymouth grow more food by using dead fish for fertilizer.

What amazes Agnes most is the amount of change in his life. One day he's a wandering man without a tribe; the next, he's a leader. She had read how the settlers depended on him to head expeditions and negotiate treaties. "Absolutely fearless," is how the book described him.

"Helloooooooooooo . . ." moans a ghostly voice.

Agnes looks up. There is *nobody* there. *Oh, well.* She picks up her paintbrush and dips it in red, then white, then orange. *How do you make that watermelon color?* she wonders. She dips the paintbrush back in the red and—

"Helllooooooooooooooo . . ." moans the voice again.

Agnes jerks her head up abruptly. "Who is that?" she calls out.

"I am the talking fence. . . . No! I mean I am the *ghost* of the fence. OOOOOOOOooooooh!" It sounds like a little kid's voice.

Agnes creeps toward the voice as it continues to ramble.

"First the fence died and then it came back to life. Oooooooooooh . . . And then it was haunted. Ohhhhhh! Now I am haunting yoooooooooooou . . ."

Agnes sees a knothole in the fence about three feet up from the ground with a pair of moist rubbery lips sticking through it. Agnes breaks off the stem of a zinnia and twirls the flower like a parasol, sticking it right on top of the fence's lips. "And I am brushing the fence's teeth . . ." drones Agnes in her own ghostly voice. "The fence's *haunted* teeth . . . ooooooooOOOOOOOOhh . . ."

The lips withdraw from the knothole. Agnes hears spitting. She peeks through the hole, making sure not to get too close in case something pops out and pokes her in the glasses. She sees an emerald square of lawn, an aluminum bench, and a brown bird-pooped statue of St. Francis holding seeds in his outstretched hand. And a tennis shoe—the kind with a rubber cap toe and Velcro fasteners. "Hey, little kid!" says Agnes. "You okay?"

She did not mean to scare him. This time, she puts her lips up to the knothole. "Hey, yoooouuuu! Pick a flower. Brush *my* teeth. It's your turn. . . . Come on. I won't bite. Oooooooohhhhh . . ." She tries to stick her lips out to the other side as far as possible. When that does not get any results, she makes loud smacking noises. "Kiss the fence," she groans hauntingly, "for the fence looooooooooves you. . . ."

"This is a weird fence."

This is not a little kid's voice. And it is coming from directly above her. She keeps her lips pressed up against the fence a little longer. She decides to try for a *Who, me?* look but can feel that her blush is a little too deep for that. She stands up and wipes her mouth with the back of her sleeve.

Joe Waldrip is hanging over the top of the fence. His black shiny hair is too short to fall forward. He laughs. "I think you scared Charlie," he says. "My little brother."

"Sorry," she says. "I didn't mean to." *Can I just run away?*

"Is this something you do all the time?"

Agnes likes that he is raising that one eyebrow. He is staring as if he finds her funny, but a little crazy. "No. Really. *He* started it . . ."

"He is a nutty little boy," says Joe frankly.

"How did you get up there?" says Agnes. "I don't remember you being this tall."

"Standing on a chair," he says. "Whatcha doing over there?" He shakes his head in the direction of Agnes's art table.

"I'm working on my Indian costume. I'm Squanto, and I have to carry a basket of fish."

"I don't know what I'm gonna do," he says.

"I thought you were Chief Joseph. Isn't he your great-grandfather or something?"

"Yep," he says.

"Won't your parents help you? I'll bet they know a lot about him."

"My dad doesn't know too much, I think." He blinks a few times. "My mom knew all about him."

Okay, thinks Agnes. *The mom is gone. But where?* Should she ask?

"My mom died," says Joe.

"Man," says Agnes. What else is there to say? Sometimes—but only once in a while—she will allow herself to peek at a thought that awful.

Joe stands with his arms dangling over the fence. It is impossible for Agnes to read his expression. "Have you started your costume yet?" she asks.

"Nope," he says.

"Boy, you don't have much time," says Agnes, and regrets it immediately. She sounds like a nag or a priss or a . . . mother.

"Don't I know it!" says Joe.

"Do you have an encyclopedia?"

"My grandma has a million *National Geographics*. I think she collects them."

"Listen. Why don't you come over? I can get the encyclopedia online. And you can print out whatever you want. . . ."

"Really?"

"Yeah. Hop over," says Agnes.

Joe hops! He clears the fence in a single leap.

And now he is standing here before her, wearing baggy jeans, a T-shirt, and a worn blue-plaid flannel shirt over everything like a kind of jacket. Why don't they have any word like *beautiful* for boys? *Handsome* seems just not *enough,* somehow. He follows her through the yard, her, Agnes. *Joe is walking with me, Joe is coming over to my house. . . .*

As she leads him through the sliding glass doors to the den, she feels shy. Now that *he's* here, it occurs to her that the plain old den might actually reveal something private about her. After all, this is the room where she lies on the floor and watches TV. Where, until recently, she made forts out of blankets. A place she sometimes spends the whole of a weekend morning in her moo-cow pajamas. As she pulls up a chair for Joe at the computer, the very chair that *she* sits in, she has a funny sensation of watching herself.

Agnes pulls up another chair and finds the *Encyclopedia Britannica* online. She types in "Chief Joseph," and immediately a black-and-white photograph appears. Chief Joseph has a wide face with sculptured-looking cheekbones, and dark, glittery eyes. His braids are tightly wrapped around and around in fabric. He wears an enormous feather headdress and a sash across his chest. Underneath the photo is the caption: "I will fight no more forever."

"My great-grandpa," says Joe.

He says it with some sadness, almost as if he had been missing him. But maybe he's joking? "I can print this out, you know," says Agnes. "You could copy the clothes in this picture."

"What about the eagle feathers?" Joe appears doubtful.

"Well, you could make those out of paper. I made fish out of paper. You can make *anything* out of paper."

"Okay. Yeah, I guess," he says, not quite convinced. "I'm not a good drawer, though."

"Well, I am," says Agnes, pleased at her own confidence. "Feathers are easy." She presses a button on the keyboard, and Chief Joseph emerges, line by line, from the printer, plus a page and a half of his story. She gathers up the pages, *smack* squares them on the table, and hands the stack to Joe. She feels like Libbo. "So, do you want to make feathers?"

"Right now?"

"Well, I already have everything in the backyard," Agnes says.

"Yeah, let's do it," says Joe with a little flash of a smile. "Let's get started."

At the patio table, Agnes draws the outline of a ten-inch feather, cuts it out carefully, and hands it to Joe.

"Just use this one as a tracer. You'll probably need to make, oh, about twenty-five more?"

Joe holds up the picture of Chief Joseph. "Yeah. About that."

Agnes watches as he carefully drags his pencil along the edge of her feather. Agnes goes back to her fish and tries not to stare as he does another, and another, completely absorbed. "After you cut them out, you can color them in with black felt pen on the tip," she explains. She slides one of his cutout feathers over to her side of the table and demonstrates. "See?" she says, holding the feather up behind her head. "Just like the picture."

And Joe smiles as if he were the happiest, sunniest person on earth. He keeps drawing, cutting, and painting for a good twenty minutes, sitting right beside her. She takes note of his funny twisted way of holding a pencil. How sometimes he stops to push up a cuff on his shirt or run his hands backward through his hair. And how he always returns to the feathers with utmost concentration. She is pretty sure he is enjoying himself.

This has got to be way different than hanging out with Neidermeyer. She is always hollering or poking him in the ribs with an elbow. Agnes even saw her do "the typewriter" on his back—something she had not seen anybody do since the fourth grade. She stood behind him in line and poked him all over with her two index fingers. Joe just stood there and laughed.

So, why me? she wonders. She is friendly with other kids but, really, Prejean has been her one and only true friend for so long. If Joe wasn't brand-new, himself, would he even give her a chance?

"I'm wearing pants, Joe." The little boy voice comes through the fence again.

"Heeeeyyyyyy . . ." says Joe back without lifting his eyes from his paper.

"Grandma bought them . . ." says the voice.

"Is that you, Charlie?" shouts Agnes.

"Joe, Grandma says come in for lunch," say Charlie's lips. "Yes, I am Charlie," he adds. Shyly.

"Be there in a minute," Joe says. He gathers up his feathers, stacking each one carefully on top of the other. "Can I come back and finish?" he asks. "Maybe tomorrow?"

"Sure. I'll be here. If you want to, just jump over."

"Great," says Joe. He pulls up a lawn chair to the fence, smiles at her, leaps, and disappears.

Agnes stares at the blue air where Joe used to be. She lays a hand on his pile of feathers and stays that way for a good long time, until—*Oh, no.* What time is it?

Agnes runs to the phone and presses Prejean's number. The tones sound a little like "Mary Had a Little Lamb," but she dials so fast that the song sounds frantic.

"Hello, Duval residence," says Prejean's mother. She has a cool lilting accent she acquired as a child growing up on a Caribbean island.

"This is Agnes. Has Prejean left yet?"

"I believe she went back to the garage to get her bike. But that was a while ago."

"Gee. I'm going to be late! Can you stop her?"

"One minute, please," sighs Mrs. Duval in a way that makes Agnes remember she did not say "please." Mrs. Duval *always* notices things like that.

Agnes feels restless just sitting here with a silent phone to her ear as it gets later and later. Finally she hears footsteps. *Hurry, Mrs. Duval. Please.*

"Agnes? I'm afraid Prejean is already gone. I couldn't catch her."

"Okay. *Thank you very much.*" Agnes says this deliberately and slowly, then hangs up. She scurries out to the backyard, then carries two paint-wet fish at a time inside to the bathroom until the tub is filled with them. The rest of her supplies she throws on top of her bed.

Seconds later she is outside, fumbling with the chain on her bicycle. It is always slipping off the gears. Agnes's paint-stained hands are now blotched with grease. *There! Fixed.* She is in too much of a hurry to hunt for her helmet. Her parents are out front digging around in the yard. She slips out the back and is off.

Agnes pumps and pumps the pedals for maximum

speed. Her turns are steep-angled. She whizzes past every familiar landmark along the way: the corner house with the scraggly grass no one ever mows; the fire hydrant someone painted to look like a spotted dog; Mr. Hahn's little store. The backstop is coming into view—at last! But where is Prejean?

"Agnes!" yells Prejean from somewhere. *"Agnes!"*

Agnes looks to her right and sees Prejean on her bike, waving and circling the lower parking lot. *"Hey!"* yells Agnes, raising her hand to wave back, when . . . *thud!* The bike stops suddenly, but Agnes's body just keeps going forward, over the handlebars. Moving in slow motion, she feels no fear. Then the pavement zooms closer to her face, and then she sees a shower of sparks on a field of black.

When Agnes opens her eyes, Prejean's face is hovering over her, streaked with tears. The whole world appears to be hazy around the edges. Is this what an angel sees when she crash-lands from heaven?

"Oh, thank God!" says Prejean, placing her hand on Agnes's shoulder.

"Where, where am I?" says Agnes, trying to joke.

"You are here at the baseball diamond," says Prejean, totally serious. "You ran into the curb. Look. I have your glasses and they are perfectly okay. I found them way over by that tree! I thought you weren't going to wake up," she says, swallowing hard.

Agnes lifts herself up on her elbow and feels her scalp. Then she touches her cheek lightly with her right hand and winces. When she stretches out her left hand for her glasses, however, she sees that she is not all right. Her hand is swollen and pulsing with pain.

"I don't have any change. I can't make a call. I'm trying to think what to do . . ." Prejean keeps patting Agnes on the back. Agnes feels a little confused by the desperation in her friend's voice.

"Can't you just call the operator? I don't think you need money for that," says Agnes.

"Yes! Yes!" says Prejean. "I don't want to leave, but I'll have to ride over to the phones. Let's move you over to the grass and you just sit, okay?"

Agnes picks herself up and notes that blood is running down her knee. Dozens of places where she hurt herself are starting to speak up, tingling and throbbing. Her swollen hand is growing larger and larger.

"I'm going to get your mom and dad. Right away."

Agnes sits quietly on the grass. Soon her father's van pulls up, and she sees her mother's panicked face through the car window, and watches as the door flies open. When she is in her mother's arms, Agnes starts to shake and, finally, begins to cry.

CHAPTER SIX

"THERE ARE FISH IN THE BATHTUB," says Mr. Parker. His face is stubbly, his hair is a haystack, and he is wearing his favorite old terry cloth bathrobe. Someone who did not know him might think he was sleepwalking.

"Really!" says Mrs. Parker, handing him a cup of coffee. "Did they swim out of the faucet?"

"No," he says matter-of-factly. "They're paper."

"They're mine," says Agnes. She has a gauze pad the size of her palm stuck to her knee with white tape. One eye is slightly swollen, and the cheek beneath it is streaked with what the nurse called road rash. And on her left hand, extending halfway up her left forearm like a clunky evening glove, is a lavender-tinted cast.

"Good choice, honey!" Mrs. Parker had said last night in the emergency room. "Lavender goes with *everything.* . . ."

Agnes will have to wear the cast for six weeks and thought that maybe this watery purple would be more interesting to live with than plain white. Now she is not so sure.

"Well, what did you have in mind?" says Mr. Parker. "Were you going to float them?"

Agnes has to smile. "No, Dad. They are for my American Indian project. Squanto, remember?"

"Oh, right." Mr. Parker obviously does not remember, even though the project has been discussed in his presence frequently. "I'm going to take a shower," he says. As he passes her in the doorway, he kisses her flat on the top of her hair. "Take care of that head," he says. "Wear a helmet next time—*every* time."

Mrs. Parker folds her arms and gives Agnes "the eye." Agnes sighs and returns the look.

"Did I say anything?" asks Mrs. Parker. "I figure you learned 'the helmet lesson' the hard way."

Agnes does not mention that wearing a helmet would not have saved her hand. Thank goodness it is her left hand.

Agnes pours herself a glass of orange juice from a carton sitting by the kitchen sink. As she sips, she sees the top of Joe's head appear over the backyard fence and disappear. Seconds later, he bobs up again. When he catches sight of her in the kitchen window, he waves!

Agnes waves back. Joe jumps the fence. *My gosh, it is only 7:30.* She is bruised, groggy, uncombed, and pajamaed. As Joe makes his way to her kitchen window, she considers making a dash for her room. She runs her good hand through her hair.

When Joe gets close enough to see the condition of Agnes's face, he stops. He draws back a little. He points to his own eye and says, "What happened?"

Agnes hold up her lavender cast for him to see. Joe covers his mouth, as if to say "Oh no!" He gestures to the sliding glass door.

Yes, she is going to greet Joe looking just like this. "Would you like to come in for a cup of coffee?" Agnes asks.

"Uh . . ." says Joe.

"Just kidding," says Agnes. She invites him in. They stand facing each other.

"Look at your knee," says Joe. They both look down at Agnes's bare leg with the yellow and purple bumps.

"Yeah," says Agnes, closing her bathrobe tight. "I crashed into a curb at the baseball field. Stupid."

"On your bike?" asks Joe. He touches the lavender cast lightly with one finger. "Does it hurt?"

"Not really," says Agnes. "I broke a bone in my hand,

but they still have to give me this big old thing."

"I didn't know they made purple casts."

"I asked for it," Agnes says. "I thought it might be an interesting color to live with."

"White is boring," agrees Joe. "I like this one." He gives her cast one soft knock.

I love it when you knock on my cast, is what Agnes wants to say. "I'm going to get dressed," is what she really says.

"Okay," says Joe, plopping down on the sofa. Then he stands up again. "Oh, do you still want to work on our stuff today? I mean, *can* you work?"

"Yep," says Agnes. "Still got my drawing hand." She turns and limps away feeling a little dizzy.

Appearing at school with a black eye, a limp, and a cast is like showing up wearing new glasses. Everyone stops and notices. Explaining what happened, however, takes a lot more time. Even when Agnes, herself, is not giving her story about crashing into the curb, she can hear somebody nearby saying, "She crashed at the baseball field." "She broke her hand and passed out." "I heard she almost got mowed down by a truck."

At first recess Agnes is surprised to be approached by a Neidermeyer with an unscrunched eye—and no sign of a sneer! *What gives?*

"Hey, Parker," says Neidermeyer. "Did you swallow

your tongue?" She says this reverently, as if she might just be deeply impressed.

"What do you mean?" Agnes asks.

"When you had your concussion. Tch." Neidermeyer tosses her head and looks at Carmella, rolling her eyes.

Prejean answers. "Actually, she did! She told me it was delicious."

Agnes joins in with a lip smacking, "Mmmmmm, *gooood tongue . . .*"

Carmella says to Agnes, "I see they have special casts for nerds now."

Agnes considers using her "special cast" to whack Carmella on the head.

"If they had special casts for idiots," Prejean says, "then you would have one covering your *entire body*."

Good one, thinks Agnes. Prejean is always so great at this kind of thing.

"Watch it, girl," Neidermeyer says.

"Yeah, watch it, girl," says Carmella.

"Let's shoot hoops with Joe," says Neidermeyer, turning on her heel.

"You know what?" says Prejean. "I think it is time to stop being so afraid of her. She is no big deal. Everyone just thinks she is."

Prejean has *never* had Neidermeyer throw a dodge ball at her head.

Agnes has to skip PE, but is just as happy to pretend

to read a book while she spies on Joe. He is going through his usual rounds, playing ball, lunching with Neidermeyer and Carmella. *You would never know that he spent practically the whole weekend with* me.

Even now, while he makes his way to the pencil sharpener, he walks right by her desk as if he does not even recognize her. She sits and listens to him grinding the sharpener behind her, feeling crushed.

Then she hears this: "I think you dropped something." It is Joe, smiling, one eyebrow raised. He hands her a pen and walks away.

It's a broken pen with the clicker missing. It doesn't even have a ballpoint. Absentmindedly, Agnes unscrews it, takes the thing apart, and sees a note inside! *Can you come over to my house after school,* it says, *for a surprise?* Yes, yes, yes! She grins, and quickly slips the note inside her desk.

Agnes has rung the Waldrips' front doorbell only once before, to sell Girl Scout cookies. The door opens— but just a few inches.

"What?" says Charlie. He is black-haired and round-faced and must look a lot like Joe did years ago. He can't be more than six years old.

"Is Joe here?"

"Joe!" he screams. As he stands and stares at her through the crack, he runs his hand back and forth

over his head. "My hair feels like grass today," he says solemnly.

Agnes reaches in cautiously and pats the glossy spikes of his hair. Is this what Joe's hair feels like?

"I'm going to cut it," he says. Agnes yanks back her hand and Charlie slams the door.

Agnes can hear Joe undoing the chain and saying, "Man, Charlie, you don't have to lock everything. What is it with you?" The door opens wide, and Joe motions her to come in.

"I think Charlie just told me he's going to cut his own hair," says Agnes.

"Oh yeah. It's his new thing. He uses this little plastic lawn mower. I think it was one of those hamburger toys," says Joe. "You know, he *pretends*. . . ."

Agnes steps into the living room. Everything looks clean and comfortable, but the furniture is old—like something out of *The Brady Bunch*. "My grandma went to get milk at the grocery store," says Joe. "So I'm baby-sitting."

"Where is your dad?" asks Agnes.

"Um, I think looking for a job."

"What happened to his old job?" asks Agnes.

"He had to quit when we moved," says Joe. "Hey, I want to show you something." He points down the hall. "This way."

In Joe's bedroom there are bunk beds with plaid spreads, matching dresser drawers, and some old model airplanes. Agnes tries to memorize everything so she can think about things later. She wonders which bunk is his. She keeps her arms folded tightly, fighting the urge to touch his things.

Cardboard boxes are stacked everywhere. They are labeled *My Room, Charlies Toys, Joes Junk, Books J. Bedroom*. Joe scoots a box across the floor with his foot. "This is the one I want," he says. He rips the tape from the top, digs in, and pulls out a soft wool blanket with black stitching around the edges. He unfolds it and holds it before her. It is beautiful, brown and orange and cream with dark red arrowheads in a pattern at the center. "It's a Pendleton blanket," he says. "And this is a real Indian design from the Northwest." He hands it to Agnes. "For Squanto," he says. "Don't you need a blanket?"

"You mean I can use this?" says Agnes. "Is it okay with your . . . dad?"

"This is *my* blanket," he says.

Agnes wraps the warm, amazing colors around her. "Look, you can't even see my cast!" she says. "Um, thank you, Joe."

"I'm just glad I could find it. I can never find anything anymore," he says.

In the half-open closet, Agnes sees tennis shoes strewn around the floor and a few stuffed animals. "When are you going to unpack?" asks Agnes.

"Uh, not just yet," he says.

"Don't you need your stuff?"

Joe shrugs.

"What happened to your mom?" She cannot believe that she has said this. But she knows, just knows, that the blanket she has wrapped around her shoulders right now belonged to Joe's mother.

"She died," says Joe.

"How?" says Agnes more quietly.

Joe closes his eyes and presses his lips together. It is so awful for Agnes to watch that she tries an easier question.

"What was her name?"

Joe opens his eyes, looks straight at her, and says, "Nora."

There is a slamming of the front door. "Grandma? Is that you?" calls Joe over his shoulder.

"No, it's me."

Joe's father appears, leaning all his weight against the bedroom doorway. He wears a rumpled dark blue suit and a loosened red tie. His face is ash-colored and his expression looks beaten. "I'm going to bed," is all he says, and he walks away.

It is as if all the air has been sucked out of the room. "Uh-oh," she whispers. "What's wrong?"

Joe turns to her. He gives a little cough—or is it a laugh?

"Maybe I shouldn't be here?" she says.

Without a word, Joe walks her out through the living room. Someone has closed the drapes, and Charlie is sitting on the sofa, absentmindedly rolling his doll-size lawn mower across his forehead. His eyes are on the television, but the volume is so low, she doubts he can hear the cartoon. He doesn't look up. Joe opens the door, and she steps outside. But before she can think of anything to say, Joe speaks. "He sleeps a lot," he says. It is the same flat, tired voice she just heard his father use. He tries a smile, then he shuts the door.

Agnes takes the blanket off, making sure it does not touch the ground. She folds it carefully and breathes in and out. Then she breaks into a dead run and she does not stop until she is safe behind the door of her very own house.

CHAPTER SEVEN

TODAY IS THE FRIDAY before Halloween. "Agnes!" Mrs. Parker is standing at the foot of the stairs with a half slip of paper in her hand. "Why didn't you tell me?"

"What?" says Agnes. She has been up since six a.m. testing her memory for her report today.

"It says right here that parents can come to your class for your presentations. Why didn't you tell me?"

"I forgot," says Agnes.

"Well, I'm coming. I'll have to make a few phone calls, but I *am* coming!"

Agnes remembers that her mother once suggested how not to be so afraid in front of an audience. She said that a very old trick was to picture the audience in their underwear. But Agnes's stagestruck brain became so scrambled, she could only picture *herself* standing there in her underwear. So Agnes has found a better solution: She pretends to give her speech just to Prejean, instead. And it works!

Agnes runs to her room and checks to see if she has forgotten anything. There is a headband with two paper feathers. Her written report. A willow basket stacked with beautiful paper fish. And, folded neatly, Joe's incredible blanket. She runs to the driveway where her mother is unlocking the van's back door.

"That boy is so sweet!" Mrs. Parker says when she sees the blanket. "How thoughtful. Here, let's put it in a paper bag."

"I think this was his mom's," Agnes says.

Mrs. Parker strokes the lovely colors. "Well, that is even sweeter, then."

Mrs. Parker starts the car as Agnes asks, "How can it be? How can your mom die and you *never* cry?"

"Are you talking about Joe?" asks Mrs. Parker. "How do you know he never cries?"

"I guess I don't really. Didn't you cry when your dad died?" asks Agnes.

Mrs. Parker turns off the ignition. "Of course, honey," she says. "But not in front of anyone."

"If you died," says Agnes, "I would cry every time someone said your name."

"Maybe," says Mrs. Parker. She squeezes Agnes's arm. "But maybe there is such a thing as hurting so much, you can't even cry. Sometimes it's hard to get started."

How can you not "get started" crying over your dead mother? thinks Agnes.

"When my dad died, I was a year younger than Joe," says Mrs. Parker. "I cried for one day, and then I stopped. You know why?"

Agnes shakes her head.

Mrs. Parker starts counting off on her fingers. "Because my sister was already crying all the time. And my mother found out that Daddy had no insurance, so we had no money. And then my mother had to get a horrible job answering a switchboard, and she was almost fired every day. No one was ever home anymore. We stopped buying things. People teased us about our clothes. The refrigerator was almost always empty . . ." Mrs. Parker's eyes soften with tears.

"Mom," says Agnes.

"See? I can cry now, sort of. Because it is over. Do you see? Oh, my poor old mom," says Mrs. Parker, collecting herself, dabbing her eyes. "We are so darned lucky, Agnes. Lucky, lucky, lucky." She starts the ignition and backs out of the driveway.

Agnes didn't mean to make her mother cry. Still, she's glad that she trusted her enough to talk that way—like she was a grown-up.

• • •

At school Neidermeyer and Carmella have started a new "Squanto!" whispering campaign. Really, it was the last thing Agnes expected. Nobody had mentioned it for ages. And on top of that, Agnes now likes Squanto, and his name has completely stopped sounding funny to her.

"Neidermeyer's a jerk," says Prejean.

"Hey, she's making fun of me, not you," says Agnes.

"Yes," says Prejean, folding her arms. "But it bugs *me,* too, you know."

No one will make fun of Prejean in her costume, thinks Agnes. She will be wearing a man's striped shirt and vest, a scarf tied around her curly dark hair, and big gypsy-looking earrings. Sequoia knew his fashion. She looks beautiful in this outfit.

"How do you like this blanket?" asks Agnes. She holds open her paper bag and lets Prejean take a peek. "Can you believe it? Isn't Joe nice?"

"Mm-hmm," says Prejean.

"Have you seen him anywhere?" Agnes continues. "I'm sort of worried about him after yesterday. You see, this weird thing happened when I was over at his house . . ."

"Nope, haven't seen him," says Prejean, bending over to pick up a wad of paper that has just ricocheted off Agnes's shoe. She picks it up, unfolds it, and shows it to Agnes. *Squanto!!!* is scrawled in red ink.

"Okay. *Now* what are you going to do?" says Prejean.

"About what?" asks Agnes. Just then Brian and Jay whisper *"Squanto!"* in her ears (one on each side) and run away.

"You can't just let everyone pick on you like this," says Prejean.

"I'm not *letting* people pick on me."

"Well, yes, you sort of are," says Prejean.

Agnes waits in the silence for Prejean to add something. Anything.

Prejean closes her eyes tightly. "I'm sorry, Agnes," she says. "I just get so mad sometimes that I have to get mad *for* you."

"Well, that's just you," says Agnes. "I never ask you to do that."

"You do so," says Prejean, jutting her chin. "You ask for it in a million different ways."

"Name one," says Agnes.

"Well . . ." says Prejean, "for one thing, whenever someone says something you don't like—you look at *me*. At *me*! Like *I'm* always supposed to say something and make all the bad people go away! Puh-leez! That's soooo *babyish*."

"*Oh yeah?* Oo, I'm sorry. I never knew it was so *hard* for you to be my friend." Agnes's voice rises. "Don't you ever get tired of being Little Miss Perfect Pants and reading everybody's thoughts and being queen of the universe and acting, you know . . . *exactly like your mother*?"

Prejean's jaw drops. "I can't *believe* you said that."

"Well, there are things about me that you wouldn't believe and that you don't know about," says Agnes hotly. "I do brave things. In fact, I did a really, really brave thing just a couple of weeks ago. *In secret!*"

"Oh, really?" says Prejean as if she were humoring a crazy person. "Makes it kind of hard to prove, doesn't it?"

Prejean turns her back and begins to walk away. And then Agnes does it. She reaches out with her good hand and—*thwap!*—snaps Prejean's bra strap like a giant rubber band.

"Ow!" Prejean winces. She reaches around and rubs her back.

"Prejean's got a bra!" howls Brian. He and Jay stick out their chests and walk around wiggling their hips. "Woooo-hoo!"

Agnes is horrified. Prejean shoots her a look of contempt. "Gee, Agnes. I hope that made you feel *real* brave."

As Agnes watches Prejean walk away, she can't decide whether to run after her and say she's sorry, or run after her and snap her bra strap again. Instead, she just stands there, simmering.

For the next few hours Agnes cannot shake the feeling that her world has changed. Now that she's adrift without her friend, nothing seems to faze her. Not Carmella doing that stupid laugh—her mouth all hanging open with no sound coming out. Not Brian, who has abbreviated his *Squanto!* whisperings to single snorts (which he shares with her every time he's sure Libbo isn't looking). Agnes just stares ahead.

When it is time to go to the bathroom and change into costumes, Prejean won't even look at her. Agnes stands across the room and tries to ignore her right back, but it feels like such a mean and awkward thing to do. She sticks a paper feather in her hair and she is *Squanto the wanderer. The man without a tribe . . .*

Agnes leaves the bathroom and steps out into the hallway at the exact moment Joe does. They are standing face-to-face, suddenly dressed as Native Americans. Joe has attached his feathers to a strip of red felt that Agnes found for him. The headdress trails all the way down his back. On his red felt sash across his chest, he has glued little paper emblems that tell the story of Chief Joseph's life.

"You used my idea," says Agnes.

"Yeah. It looks good, doesn't it?" He straightens the sash. He stands extra tall and extra straight so that his headdress won't fall off.

"Are you nervous?" asks Agnes.

"I'm okay," he says.

"My mom is coming," says Agnes. As soon as Joe's face falls, she adds, "How about your dad? He's coming, isn't he?"

Joe looks around impatiently. "I doubt it," he says.

In the classroom, parents are crowded at the back, looking all wrong in chairs that are too small for them. Agnes spots her mother smiling and nodding with Mrs. Duval, mother of Prejean, who once was her very best friend in all the world. Now who will she make her stupid speech to?

"Squanto!" Agnes feels the hot word in her ear. She turns to see Neidermeyer and Carmella, who salute her with a quick sticking-out of their tongues before pushing past her. (*Jerk One and Jerk Two.* Boy, she is so sick of both of them.)

Agnes takes her seat. Ashley Cardell goes first.

"I'm Pocahontas?" she begins.

She is very flashy, this Ashley Pocahontas. She is wearing pink lip gloss, plus about five pounds of turquoise jewelry.

"And so I see him and I say to my father? Who is that white man? Because I have, like, never seen a white man before? And then the guy says, 'I am John Smith!' And right away I think, like, is this love at first sight?"

Agnes cannot blame Brian for snickering. As Sitting

Bull, however, he is all business. "I am a teenage warrior," he says. "I am not afraid of *anything.*"

Such a boy, thinks Agnes. Well, Squanto wasn't a fighter, but he was no chicken, either. She pulls her blanket around her tight and sits up straight.

When Brian finishes, it is Agnes's turn. She pushes up her glasses, clutches her blanket, and stomps to the front of the class. Over the heads of her classmates, she sees her mother smiling expectantly. To her left, near the front, she sees Neidermeyer, dressed as Wovoka the Ghost Dancer. Was the real Wovoka ever such a smirker? She has her arms behind her head, her legs stretched out in the aisle. *You know what, Neidermeyer? You take up too much space.*

"Call me Squanto!" says Agnes, and takes a quick scan around the room. Carmella's and Neidermeyer's eyes are bulging as if their heads are going to explode. Agnes stares right back at them. "But that's just a nickname. My *real* name is Tisquantum. And if it wasn't for me," she says, her voice floating out, "there would be no Neidermeyer."

Neidermeyer pulls out of her sprawl and sits bolt upright. "Huh?" she says.

"That's right. *No Neidermeyer!*" The classroom starts to fill with giggles. Agnes places her basket on Mrs. Libonati's desk and pulls out a paper fish. "See this?" she says, dangling one of her shiny hand-painted trout toward Neidermeyer. "I showed your great-great-great-great-great-grandparents how to grow crops using this as fertilizer." Agnes tries hard to sound dignified, as she believes Squanto would.

"The whole *Mayflower* group was starving. They didn't know how to grow enough food to feed themselves. But I showed them. And because of me, they lived." Here Agnes pauses. "And so—you're welcome."

At this, several of the parents burst into applause and "atta girl" head nodding. One of the parents even gives a high-pitched whistle. Hearing the applause is like swallowing sunshine. Agnes feels as if its rays are streaming out of her eyes and ears. And the kids start clapping, too! And Neidermeyer, she is just looking up through her eyebrows into the middle distance, making eye contact with ·nobody. *How does it feel,* Mayflower *girl?*

The rest of her speech seems to race by. In fact, if she could figure out a way to make it last a few extra seconds, she would! When she picks up her basket and starts walking back to her desk, she finds herself suddenly shaky. Even her neck is wobbling. The internal sunshine melts into just plain fire. Such a strange, strange feeling—scary and fantastic.

Natalie Kim stands up to speak, but Agnes cannot hear a thing. She is vaguely conscious of Brian poking her on the arm, saying ha-ha. Then she can't focus on

Pat Marie's speech, either. She is mesmerized by what *she* did, what *she* said. Ohmigosh. Where did *that* come from?

It is not until Joe stands up that Agnes regains her calm. She pushes her thoughts away and, with a deep, inner stillness, concentrates on him.

Joe checks his headdress, gives it a tap to make sure it isn't falling off. He drops his hands to his sides, takes a deep breath, and says: "I am Chief Joseph, leader of the Nez Perce tribe . . ."

Then his eyes fix on the back of the room. Agnes turns. And there, shutting the classroom's back door as quietly as he can, is Mr. Waldrip. He is wearing jeans and a soft-looking shirt. He is trying to smile at Joe, nodding his head as if to say "Keep going."

Agnes turns back to Joe. He appears completely lost. "I am Chief Joseph," Joe starts again, "leader of the Nez Perce tribe . . ."

He has practiced this speech with Agnes. *I fought for my people.* . . . Agnes wills Joe to remember the next line.

Joe closes his eyes, mouths some words under his breath. "I fought for my people. I fought long and hard. So it is, it is funny . . ."

Say it, Joe, Agnes wants to shout.

"It is funny," continues Joe, "what people remember about me." He stops, gives a little half-laugh. He looks at the floor and shakes his head from side to side, then freezes.

Agnes says, *"Psst!"* and waves, trying to capture his attention so she can feed him a line, anything . . .

But when Joe looks up, he gazes to the back of the room and says, hoarsely, "I will fight no more forever." He reaches up, drops his headdress to the floor, marches steadily past all the students in the front row, opens the classroom door, and walks out.

Brian turns to Agnes and says, "Was that *it*?" The whole class starts buzzing.

Agnes cannot *believe* that everyone is just sitting there. She stands up and weaves through the aisles past faces looking up at her in wonder. Mrs. Libonati says, "Agnes!" as she rushes out the door.

There in the hallway, Joe is wrapped in the arms of his father. Joe lets himself be hugged but then pulls back and hits his father in the chest with his fist. His father lets himself be hit, then draws him back. Joe makes a sound. A low note. He does it again and again. He is crying.

Agnes feels a hand on her shoulder. Her mother says, "Agnes, come inside," softly but firmly. Not knowing what else to do, Agnes follows her mother.

My gosh. *Poor Joe.*

CHAPTER EIGHT

"I SHOULD HAVE KNOWN!" said Tiff. "The personality changes! The mood swings. . . . All signs of infection by an Aurelian virus."

"Yeah," says Zori. "I hate it when that happens."

"Well, next time I'll give you the benefit of the doubt!" says Tiff, swinging her blond and magenta hair.

"Until there's a cure for it," says the dark, leather-clad Zori, "I'm afraid you'll have to."

Guitar Girls of Planet Z is almost eerie.

An alien virus takes over Zori's body and causes a complete personality change. Which leads to all sorts of misunderstandings and a big fight between Zori and best friend Tiff.

Agnes hovers by the phone. Will Prejean make her traditional call? To top it off, tomorrow is Halloween! Will Agnes really have no one to trick-or-treat with? Would she really dare going door-to-door all by herself? *Ring, phone! Ring!*

Agnes stares down the phone until her mother says it is time to go. She checks twice to make sure the answering machine is on before she leaves for the art supply store.

She is planning to be the Ace of Hearts—just like the playing cards in *Alice in Wonderland*. All she needs are two sturdy pieces of cardboard, ribbon to tie the cards at her shoulders, a little red paint . . . She decides to buy extra cardboard for Prejean, just in case. Prejean doesn't like to draw or paint, and they *had* talked a little about being Hearts and Diamonds together only last week. And then, when Prejean calls, she can say: *Of course I forgive you. In fact, I'm working on your costume right now!*

All the way home her mother keeps stopping to do errands—the grocery store, the dry cleaners. And all the while Prejean could be calling, calling . . . Agnes bolts from the car as soon as it stops rolling. To the answering machine!

The happy red light is blinking. Agnes raises her hands and says, *"Yes!"* She can't rewind the tape fast enough.

"AGnees parKER. This is the Harvard Public Library. Your copy of *SQUANTOHISLIFEANDTIMES* is over-due. . . ."

It's nothing but a stupid, phone-calling library robot! Agnes waits to see if . . .

"There are no more messages."

If Prejean is that mad, well . . . Couldn't Agnes make the call? She picks up the phone and dials. "Hello?" says Prejean.

Prejean's voice sounds almost . . . perky. It's not the voice of someone who has been sitting around worrying about Agnes. Agnes hangs up.

Maybe Prejean is conducting some sort of test, thinks Agnes. Maybe she's sitting there smiling, just waiting for her babyish, wishy-washy friend to *beg* her to come back. *Well—forget it!*

In order to avoid the temptation to call again, Agnes decides to get as far away from the phone as possible. She gathers up all her supplies and lays everything out on the patio table. She folds a piece of paper in half and traces out half of a heart. It is hard drawing smooth lines because she is shivering.

She puts down her pencil and is blowing on her fingers when she hears, "What's up?"

"Joe?" she says. She climbs up on a chair to see over the fence. There he is, peering up at her.

"Hi," he says.

Agnes says, "Uh, how is everything over there?"

"It's okay," says Joe. Then he immediately adds, "Did you tell people?" He is not smiling, and he is motionless.

"Of course not," she says.

"Really?"

"I would never tell anyone. Never."

"Good," says Joe. He rubs his hands up and down his arms to warm himself. Has he been waiting out here a long time hoping to catch a glimpse of her and ask her that question?

"I'll tell you something, though," says Agnes. "Neidermeyer talked a lot about you. She kept saying how cool you were."

"How's that?" says Joe.

"She said you were cool to walk out on your speech. She thinks you were mad, or something."

Joe wrinkles his nose. "Peggy said that?"

Peggy? He must be the only person in the world who calls her that. "She says you left because, uh, you don't like your dad."

"I like my dad," Joe says firmly.

"Of course," says Agnes.

"He's having trouble," says Joe.

"Yeah," says Agnes.

"My mom, she died too fast," Joe says.

Agnes nods her head, though she does not really understand what he means.

"She was supposed to get treated for . . . her cancer."
He winces.

There. He said it.

"But then everything went too fast. All of a sudden he decides we should move, and then he quits his job and we get rid of our house. I still don't know why. Maybe he thought Grandma would help take care of us."

"And she does that, right?" says Agnes.

"Well, yeah. But then Dad started sleeping *all* the time. And I don't think any of us knows what to do about *that*."

"Is he sick?" says Agnes.

"Maybe, but he's trying not to be. At least that's what he said," says Joe. "Doesn't exactly make any sense, does it?"

"It's good he's trying to get better," says Agnes. "But you know what else?"

"What?" says Joe.

"Well, it's good he's talking to you about it. Don't you think? Like, my dad doesn't talk a lot. And even though he's a good dad, it would be weird to be alone with just him. Especially if you needed any actual information."

"Yes!" says Joe. *"Exactly."* He seems amazed, as if Agnes had read his mind.

This admiration makes Agnes suddenly shy. "Man, your lips are blue," she says.

Joe wraps his arms around himself and hops up and

down a few times. "I gotta go in," he says. "I'm freezing!"

"Me, too," says Agnes. "And I'm wearing a sweatshirt!"

"I'll see ya, Agnes," Joe says.

"See ya, Joe," says Agnes. She watches him run into the house. It is October 30, the first day she ever heard Joe say her name!

To add to the chill this Halloween night, the clouds have thickened and the wind is jostling the dead leaves from the trees. Agnes is wearing waffley long johns under everything. Mrs. Parker has Agnes stand in front of the giant lighted pumpkin she carved earlier that day. "Smile!" she says, and aims the camera.

Agnes does her best.

"Well, it's just too bad that Prejean has the flu," says Mrs. Parker.

"Yes, it is," says Agnes, trying to look sympathetic.

"Are you sure you don't want me to go with you? I'll walk twenty-five steps behind you . . ." says Mrs. Parker.

"I'm absolutely sure," says Agnes decisively. Geez, that's all she needs. To be seen trick-or-treating with her mommy!

"Make sure to use your flashlight!" Mrs. Parker calls out after her.

As soon as she steps outside, a crazy wind starts, stops, changes direction, and slaps at her. Agnes's hanging cardboard Ace of Hearts lifts right up. No sooner does she reach back to hold it down than the card in front is raised by another gust. And she is already carrying the sack and a flashlight. This is going to be a challenge for a girl with a cast.

Agnes looks around for some kids she might know. She half expects to see Prejean just walking along with a big happy group. If only she had worn a costume with a mask, instead. Anyway, she's glad she started out late. The streets are crowded, and there are lots of packs of kids to follow up to each doorway.

She has trick-or-treated for about three blocks when she comes to one of the most popular houses in the neighborhood. It's a mob scene. Kids are crowding the beautiful brick walkway and spilling over on the lawn. The porch is lined with ten perfect pumpkins. The shrubs are covered with store-bought spiderwebs, and there are light-up tombstones on the lawn and a mechanical Frankenstein whose head pops up and down in the picture window.

Even the door mat is in on the ghoulish act. *"Whahahahahhahhahah!"* it laughs as soon as you step on it.

The lady at the door is wearing a hoop skirt and a big straw garden hat. "Candy, y'all?" she says. She holds a silver tray stacked with a gleaming assortment of full-size candy bars. Agnes reaches in, grabs a Kit Kat, and quickly says thank you before being pushed from behind. What a contrast to the house next door. It doesn't even have a porch light on. Agnes follows some kids who are with their father to the front step.

"Trick or treat!" they cry when a lady appears. She is tiny, not any bigger than a child. In fact, Agnes might even be taller. She is using one of those four-legged walkers.

"Oh, you all look so nice and scary!" she says. "But I am so sorry. I don't have any candy this year. I just couldn't get out . . ."

"Candy!" shouts a little boy.

"I promise everyone to have lots of wonderful candy next year," says the lady. She grins, showing a row of tiny, perfectly shaped, impossibly white upper teeth.

"Can you say happy Halloween to this nice lady?" asks the father.

"Candy!" shouts the boy.

"Happy Halloween," says Agnes. She watches as the lady slowly backs her walker out of the door. It has to take a lot to shut the door, sit down, get up, open it again. All to announce that there won't be any candy to a bunch of disappointed kids.

Agnes straggles over the front lawn when another group of trick-or-treaters approaches: a bunch of preschoolers, each with one arm above the head, walking hand-in-hand with a parent. Some of the children are so young, they look confused—as if someone woke them up in the middle of the night just to put them in funny clothes.

"Excuse me," says Agnes. "This lady isn't giving out candy. And it's really hard for her to get to the door . . ."

A mother in a big hooded sweatshirt gives her a wave. "Okay, sweetie. Thanks for telling us," she says. With effort they get the group of little kids turned around and head off in another direction. Even while holding their parents' hands, they all manage to bump into one another.

Agnes stops and thinks. Thanks to the house next door, there are going to be tons of kids knocking and ringing. Maybe she could rip off part of her costume and make a little sign?

"Trick or treat! Smell my feet! Give me something good to eat!"

Agnes startles, then turns around. *Oh, rats . . .*

Neidermeyer, dressed as a pirate, hits herself on the chest and belches. Carmella shrieks with laughter. Both have hooks and eye patches. And in between the two is Joe! As he draws closer, Agnes sees that he has black circles under his eyes, ripped clothes, and tire tracks on his T-shirt.

"Hey, Joe," Agnes says. "What're you supposed to be?"

"Um, roadkill?" says Joe.

"*My* idea!" says Neidermeyer. She raises her hook hand in the air and belches again. Carmella laughs just as hard.

"Look at how much candy you have," says Agnes to Joe, doing her best to ignore the burping pirate.

"We started at five-thirty," says Joe.

"We are *always* first," sniffs Carmella.

"I think a lot of people weren't ready for us," says Joe.

"Oh, so what? How tough is it to break open a bag of candy?" says Neidermeyer. "And you, *Ace*," she says, turning to Agnes, "why don't you *shuffle* off? I'm gonna get me some more booty!" She shakes her pillowcase. "Arrrgh!" she says.

"Not here, Neidermeyer," says Agnes.

Neidermeyer stops, draws in her chin, slaps her hand on her hip. "Oh, yeah?" she says. "We'll do exactly—"

"Listen," Agnes cuts her off. "There is a little old lady living here and she doesn't have any candy. Just go next door. They have lots. Full-size Kit Kats." She pulls a candy bar out of her bag. "See?"

Neidermeyer takes this back talk too calmly. "No treats, huh? That's *too* bad," she says with a fakey sweetness. "Then it's time for a *trick*!" She reaches into the pocket of her black sweatpants and pulls out a jumbo egg. She holds it up and examines it like a jeweler. "Grade A!" she exclaims.

"Oh, *come* on!" says Agnes.

Neidermeyer winds up slowly, lifting her knee like a major league pitcher. *Blam!* The egg hits the old lady's door. Bits of shell mixed with runny yolk crawl down the screen.

Agnes feels a shock go through her. "How *could* you?" she says.

Neidermeyer just smiles and pulls another egg out of her big pocket.

"Stop," says Joe.

Neidermeyer pauses and gives Joe a surprised glance. She lowers her arm for a moment, then winds up and hurls the egg directly at Agnes. Agnes ducks, but Neidermeyer nails her square in the center of her Ace of Hearts. Carmella yells, "Bull's-eye!"

Agnes looks down at the shattered egg dripping from her costume. The red paint starts to run. She is furious and speechless.

"That's *it!*" Joe takes three long steps and grabs Neidermeyer by the arm. "Give me those eggs," he says.

Neidermeyer yanks her elbow out of his grip. "No way," she says.

"I'm not leaving you alone until I get the eggs," says Joe.

"Joe, they call it *trick* or treat," says Neidermeyer slowly, as if she were a kindergarten teacher. "Get a grip! This is the *best* part."

"Just hand them over," says Joe.

Neidermeyer goes nose to nose with Joe. "Didn't you tell me just twenty minutes ago that I was the *funnest girl you ever met*?"

"Yeah. So?"

"Well, I *still am!*" Neidermeyer salutes the air with her fist. But then she studies Joe's face and sees that he's not smiling. "Sure you want this egg, chicken?" she teases. Faking a throw at Joe's head, she runs backward with the egg, her eyes glinting. When she winds up again, Agnes can see she means to pelt him good.

Joe lunges at her and they tussle. The egg drops and smashes. He tries to get his hand into her pocket for the last egg, but Neidermeyer, always a good wiggler, breaks away again and again. Suddenly Carmella sneaks up behind Joe, and whangs him with her heavy pillowcase.

"Two on one! Not fair!" shouts Agnes from the curb, just to let Joe know she's on his side.

Finally, Neidermeyer straightens up and sprints away, breaking into a wild manic laugh as she dashes into the street. But she cannot resist the temptation of looking over her shoulder and—*smack!*—smashes into a gaggle of big middle-school kids. Taken completely by surprise, she cannot recover her balance. She falls on her hip and skids along the pavement.

The middle-school crowd are boys and girls dressed

in baggy dark clothes. No costumes. Just walking around looking cool is enough. One girl with straight blond hair and a ton of eye makeup stands over the fallen Neidermeyer.

"Pathetic," she announces, then folds her arms and walks off, taking the crowd with her.

Carmella waits until the group is well down the street and then rushes to help her friend. "Are you okay?" she asks with a flinch.

She isn't, in fact. Neidermeyer is boiling. She cusses. Twice. When she picks herself up off the street, she leaves a dark slimy spot.

Agnes bursts out laughing and hops around in little circles. "Hey, Neidermeyer, what's wrong—got an omelet in your pants?" With this, Joe laughs, too.

Neidermeyer touches her gooey pocket. She gives Joe a tight little smile. "I'm getting out of here," she says. "Why don't you and Hagness Puker just hang out in dorkville for the rest of the night?"

Joe stands with Agnes and watches Neidermeyer limp away.

"There they go," says Agnes. She is half expecting that he will follow them.

Instead, Joe peeks into his giant bag of treats. "Look at all this junk," he says.

"You're lucky," says Agnes. "I have practically nothing. It's the worst Halloween I've ever had."

Just then, a shaft of light falls across the yard. The little old lady has opened her door. She stands behind the egged screen. "Oh, dear," she says. "What is this?" Her voice is trembling and she is blinking quickly.

Agnes tugs Joe's sleeve. "Come on!" she whispers. "Come with me to the door."

Up close, Agnes is struck again by how small the lady is. "Some kids threw eggs at us and they missed," says Agnes. "Look," she says, pointing to the egg smeared across her costume.

"Oh, dear," says the lady again, looking left and right like a nervous little bird.

"But they're gone now," says Joe, striding up. "We chased them off."

"Are you sure?" says the lady.

"Yeah," says Agnes. "And I'll clean up this mess."

The lady lets out a big breath. "Oh, could you? Because I really can't get to it."

"No problem. Can we use your hose?" Joe asks.

"Yes. I believe it is hanging over by those bushes on a hook." She waits as Joe scrambles through the shrubbery.

"Got it!" says Joe, holding up the nozzle so the lady can see it.

"You better go inside while we squirt it," says Agnes.

"Yes." The lady nods. "Yes, I believe I will." She slowly backs her walker from the doorway and stops. "Thank you, children," she says.

Joe props open the screen and sprays off all the muck. Agnes stations herself at the end of the driveway to warn off new trick-or-treaters. Every once in a while, she looks over her shoulder at Joe and smiles. He looks back and waves. "All clean!" he shouts.

When he's done, Joe says, "Hey, tell you what. Let's split up this candy." He dumps his sagging pillowcase on the driveway before Agnes. The hems of his jeans are soaking wet.

"Really?" says Agnes.

"Yeah. It's way too much." He turns the bag upside down and out slides a monster load. Stray wrappers get picked up by a gust of wind and scoot down the street.

"Yee-haw!" says Agnes. "That is a whole candy mountain you've got there!"

"It's a candy avalanche!" says Joe.

"Man, this is so great! Do you like Almond Joys?" asks Agnes, licking her lips.

"Hate 'em!" he says. "They're yours if you want them."

The two of them eagerly pick through the candy. Agnes loves coconut and candy corn, which is fine with Joe, who likes neither. Joe likes peanuts and caramel, so Agnes throws all those his way as they scramble through the pile.

"How about bubble gum?" burbles Agnes, her mouth stuffed with Mounds. "I love bubble gum."

"We'll split it," says Joe.

"And what do I do with this?" says Agnes, holding up a narrow yellow box.

"Oh, brother," says Joe. "Toothpaste?"

"No, I don't think so," says Agnes. She pulls her miniature flashlight from her bag and takes a closer look. *Creme D'Anchois*, it says on the box. And beneath, in smaller print, *Anchovy Paste . . . Gross!* "Maybe it's supposed to be a 'trick.' Or maybe," says Agnes, "someone out there is *crazy*."

She heaves the box at Joe, who tosses it back like a hot potato. They go back and forth, giggling, until Agnes grabs it. She presses the tube of fish paste into Joe's hand and says, "For you. A souvenir." She looks up at him. "Feel free to keep it . . . *forever!*" She says this in a goofy way, but her heart is oddly thumping. His hand is so . . .

"Prejean!" says Joe.

"Huh?" says Agnes.

"Over there, across the street. Hey, Prejean!" yells Joe.

It *is* Prejean. She's standing on a porch with a big group of kids. Agnes wants to tell Joe to quit waving.

"Hey, Agnes," says Joe. "Did you guys get separated or something?"

"Uh, yeah . . ." *In a big way*, Agnes almost adds. But then something happens: Prejean's "crowd" takes a left, and Prejean takes a right. She is alone.

101

"Prejean!" Joe yells again. "Over here!"

Prejean turns and spots Joe. Her hair is wild and wind-tangled. She is the Ace of Diamonds after all—a very crumpled Ace. The cardboard she used wasn't heavy enough. And Agnes winces when she sees the crooked red lettering in watery marker. The costume is so bad, it's kind of embarrassing.

Agnes, feeling a little stab of pity, immediately runs to meet her. "Hi," she says.

"Hi," says Prejean flatly.

"You're the Ace of Diamonds," says Agnes.

"Yeah. And *you* didn't call," says Prejean.

"*Neither* did you," she says.

"Well, I'm glad I didn't, because it looks like you had other plans . . ." She glances in Joe's direction. "You're having fun, though. I guess that's what's important."

Agnes has half a mind to turn around and leave until she notices that Prejean's eyes are taking on a shine. *My gosh.* She really is on the verge of tears! "Prejean Duval," says Agnes gently. "Why don't you know that you are my best friend in the whole stupid world?"

Prejean quickly wipes her eyes and gives a sniff. She stands tall and looks over Agnes's shoulder, trying to appear interested in something happening far away. "Yep," she says.

"I was afraid to call because, you know, you said I was a baby."

"I *never* said you were a baby."

"Well, you said I needed not to lean on you and that I *acted* like a baby. It's the same thing, isn't it? I really thought you'd call like you usually do. If you wanted to see me, I mean."

"Oh. So then you called *him*?"

"No! I was alone! I just caught up with Joe. Really. C'mon. Let's go across the street."

Prejean rolls her eyes.

"C'mon," Agnes pleads.

"Oh . . . okay," says Prejean at last. "But I have to ask: Did you see *Guitar Girls* yesterday? Wasn't that *weird*?"

"I'll say," says Agnes.

"I mean, are they psychic? How did they know *you* were suffering with the Aurelian virus?"

Me?

"*Joe this, Joe that* . . ." Prejean shakes her head. "I know he's nice, but . . ."

Agnes pulls a grumbling Prejean by the sleeve. When they get across the street, they find Joe dumping candy in the little old lady's mail slot. "Hey." He smiles. "I had some extra."

How sweet. Agnes looks over at Prejean, but her friend's expression is positively stony.

"Joe is sharing his candy tonight with everybody," says Agnes cheerily. "He gave me half his bag."

Prejean refuses to react. "So is it time to go home?" she asks.

"Probably," says Agnes, ashamed for her friend's rudeness.

"I'm ready," says Joe.

The three make their way down the sidewalk; Joe on the left, Prejean on the right, and Agnes in the middle. "Hey, Joe," she says. "Tell Prejean about Neidermeyer and the eggs."

As Joe tells the story and Prejean tries her hardest not to appear interested, Agnes can't help but wonder: *Just who is the baby in this group?* She knows the answer. But why should that make her feel so strange?

Chapter Nine

"Can I skip breakfast?" asks Agnes. She is staring at a bowl of Wheaties. Never have they appeared more un-appealing, more gloppy.

"Hmmmm," says her mother. "Could it be you already had breakfast?"

"Sort of," says Agnes.

"You know, I walked by your room this morning. The entire carpet is glittering with candy wrappers."

"Yeah," says Agnes. She folds her arms over her stomach and gives a little shudder.

Mrs. Parker rolls her eyes. "Okay. You can skip it. But you have to promise to eat a decent lunch."

Agnes nods, though the thought of eating anything

is disgusting. Especially anything with—*coconut. Ugh.* Still, it's even worse for Prejean. Her mother makes her hand over the candy bag and doles out two measly pieces a day. Better to have your entire bag all to yourself and risk a queasy stomach. Because there are about five best things in the universe, and candy is one of them! Agnes makes sure to drop an emergency Almond Joy in her lunch bag, just in case.

At school candy is the center of everyone's day. Kids smuggle it in their backpacks to eat while Libbo is not looking. Some have sandwich bags full in their desks. Agnes notices that Brian has something in his cheek practically all morning. When he lifts the top of his desk as the recess bell rings, Agnes gets a peek at a big pile of silver-and-blue foil wrappers. A definite thing for peppermint patties.

All in all this would be a good Monday, except Joe is absent. Agnes had wondered how he and Neidermeyer would hit it off today. Would she still be mad? Or had *he* finally had enough of *her*? She watches Neidermeyer at the lunch table, heckling Brian, punching him in the arm and dodging as he flings sandwich crusts at her hair. *Business as usual.*

The next day when Agnes arrives at school, there is a tight knot of kids in the breezeway, including Prejean. She spots Agnes and motions furiously for her to come over.

"It's the truth!" says Neidermeyer. "I should know. His grandma called *my* parents."

"What is she talking about?" asks Agnes.

"Joe ate poisoned candy," says Brian.

Agnes looks at Brian and says, "No way!"

"*Way*. I had to throw my whole bag out," says Neidermeyer. "The *cops* made me." She squinches up her eye when she says *cops*.

"It's *true*. They came to my house, too," says Carmella, sounding grave and trembly.

"Wouldn't this have been on the news?" asks Prejean.

"How do I know!" says Neidermeyer. "Am I in charge of the news?" She gives Prejean a look that says *Duh!*

Agnes has to speak up. "Who told you about Joe? First you said his grandma and then you said the police. Which one was it?"

Neidermeyer turns to Carmella. "*Why* is *she* talking to me?"

"*I can't hear a thing*," says Carmella innocently.

"Why would Neidermeyer lie about it?" asks Brian.

"I think it's creepy," whispers Ashley.

"Hey, Neidermeyer," says Jay. "Do they know where the candy came from?"

"All's I know is what they told me, which is to throw all my candy away."

"Should we throw away *our* candy?" asks Ashley, pale and wide-eyed.

"I don't know," says Neidermeyer, suddenly annoyed by all the questions. "But I'll tell ya one thing. I'll bet Joe wishes he threw away *his* candy."

The Joe subject is all anyone discusses after that.

"Did Neidermeyer say he was okay?" Agnes asks Prejean.

"He's in the *hospital!*" says Ashley, who has been tagging along behind.

"Oh, Prejean!" says Agnes, alarmed. *"Did I tell you about the anchovy paste!"*

"*What* paste?" says Ashley, butting in between the two of them. "Tell me, you guys!"

Prejean groans. "He wouldn't eat that. Neidermeyer's probably getting back at Joe for all that egg business," she says.

"Then why isn't Joe here today?" Agnes asks.

"Good point," says Prejean quietly.

Agnes feels sick to her stomach—and not a candy kind of sick. On one hand, Neidermeyer is a miserable liar. On the other hand, what if poor Joe is really very, very sick? Sick enough to be in a hospital?

All morning Agnes sends wishes on Joe's empty chair. "Be okay, Joe," she says. "Be okay. Be okay . . ." But it would feel so much better to actually *do* something.

Agnes opens her notebook to an empty page. In one

column she writes: *Joe missing*. In the other column she writes: *Neidermeyer changes story. Neidermeyer mad at Joe. No announcement on news.* And finally: *Joe's candy— I ate it!!*

Agnes touches her throat.

"I don't believe it," Agnes says the moment she meets up with Prejean. "And I don't care if I'm the only person in school who thinks so. She is lying." Agnes looks around at the crowded lunch benches. *"L-y-i-n-g!"* she shouts. Then she smiles and opens her lunch sack. "It'll be okay, Prejean," she says.

"I think she's lying, too," says Prejean. "But who can tell? It's driving me nuts."

"Look, no one has eaten more of Joe's candy than me, right? And am I poisoned?"

Agnes takes out her sandwich in its Ziploc bag. Beside it she places a box of orange juice. Next, out comes a bag of baby carrots. And here she pauses, rather dramatically. She looks deep into Prejean's eyes, reaches into the sack, and pulls out . . . an *Almond Joy*.

"No, Agnes!" says Prejean. "Don't!"

"Yes, Agnes," she says. "Do!"

"Please, please don't," says Prejean.

"Don't do what?" asks Ashley.

"*This*," Agnes announces, "is a piece of Joe's candy."

"Ohmigosh!" says Ashley. She elbows Natalie Kim. "Look! That's *Joe's* candy!"

Agnes holds up the candy bar for everyone's inspection.

"Ohmigosh!" says Natalie.

"And I'm gonna *eat it*!" says Agnes. "Eat it all up!"

"No, she's not," says Prejean. "She's kidding." Ashley and Natalie are already blabbing to the people behind them. "Agnes!" whispers Prejean. "I get it, okay? You're brave. But *now* isn't the time . . ."

The news reaches Brian and his gang, and they are over at Agnes's table in a flash. "Why do you have Joe's candy?" he asks.

"Because we shared," says Agnes. "And he gave me allllll his coconut candy. Didn't he, Prejean?"

"Uh-huh," says Prejean. "Now why don't you guys go sit down? She is not going to eat it."

"I'd *love* to see her eat it!" booms Neidermeyer.

Agnes's heart does a flip. Neidermeyer swaggers up and plants herself in front of her, face-to-face.

"Oh yeah?" says Agnes in the toughest voice she can muster. "Well, watch this!"

Agnes slowly tears the paper wrapper down the side of the candy bar, almost as if she is peeling a banana. All the kids stand around, hushed and waiting. When she gets down to the naked candy bar, she wags it close to Neidermeyer's face. Then Brian takes it upon himself to break the silence.

"*Eat it!*" he barks.

Some kids laugh. And gradually, the other boys join Brian in a little chant.

"Eat *it*! Eat *it*! Eat *it*!" they say, careful to keep their voices low so the lunch ladies don't get wind of this.

Agnes opens her mouth wide and lowers it over the top of the Almond Joy. Crunch! She has bitten the bar perfectly in half, right through the almond. The crowd cheers! Agnes munches, swallows, and takes another bite.

"Oh, Agnes!" says Prejean. She drops her head in her hands.

"Now that is what I call stupid," says Carmella.

"Is that so?" says Agnes, her mouth full of chocolate. She shoves the last of the candy in her mouth. Her lips bulge over her teeth and she swallows hard.

"I hope you know the number for 911!" says Neidermeyer.

"It's 9-1-1 . . ." says Agnes, very slowly. An actual Prejean-like comeback!

"Well, okay then," says Neidermeyer, momentarily flustered. "Remember it." She turns to leave, but pauses to shout over her shoulder. "And RIP, Gagness Barfer!"

"I wish you hadn't done that," says Prejean as the other kids start to leave.

"I *had* to do it," says Agnes.

Prejean sighs and shakes her head.

"I had to," Agnes insists. "*You* would've done it." She

takes her napkin and wipes her chocolatey lips. Then she sneaks out her tongue and dabs her napkin on that, too. "P-tooie," she says.

For the rest of the afternoon, Agnes is very alert to any signs of being poisoned. Is the math lesson more boring than usual, or is she slipping into a coma? Agnes waits until Libbo is busy writing grammar sentences on the board and gives Prejean a wave. She makes a face and mouths the word *barf*. Her stomach is churning.

Not good! Why didn't Agnes just stay a big chicken? As she sits through the final minutes of school, she pictures Joe dumping his candy bag over and over and over. Joe smiling. Joe reaching into his bag . . .

Brrrrrrrriiiiiiing! goes the bell.

Agnes startles. *Man, have I got to hurry!*

Prejean runs to Agnes's desk. "Are you okay?" she asks.

"I'm going to run as fast as I can to Joe's house," says Agnes. "I've got to know right now."

"Yeah. All right," says Prejean. She lowers her voice and whispers, "Because I've got to know, too."

"Don't worry," says Agnes. "Go home. I'll call. I promise."

As soon as Agnes is out of the classroom door, she is running. Her heavy backpack clunks at her and she seems to be moving slower than she has ever run before.

She begins pumping her arms, continually bumping herself in the ribs with her cast.

"Spaz!" shouts Neidermeyer as Agnes clomps by.

But Agnes truly doesn't care. She pounds pavement, rounding the corner to the Waldrips' street. Winded, sweaty, and suffering from a side ache, Agnes catches sight of Mrs. Waldrip out in her front yard, bent over a flower bed with a bamboo rake.

"Mrs. Waldrip!" says Agnes, panting. She rests her hands on her knees and tries to catch her breath. "Excuse me!"

"Yes?" says Mrs. Waldrip, clapping some dirt off her garden gloves.

"Joe here?"

"Pardon me?" says Mrs. Waldrip.

"Sorry," says Agnes, still panting too hard to make complete sentences. "I was wondering . . . where Joe is."

"Joe is not here right now," says Mrs. Waldrip, pressing her lips together.

Agnes looks at Mrs. Waldrip's face for clues. "Is he," she asks, "at the hospital?"

Mrs. Waldrip goes pale. "Oh, my goodness," she says. "How did you know?"

Agnes's heart sinks. "Neidermeyer told me," says Agnes.

"Who in the world is Neidermeyer?" says Mrs. Waldrip.

"You know, Peggy. The girl Joe went trick-or-treating with."

"Oh yes. I remember Joe saying something about a Peggy . . ."

"But I thought you called her about the poison," says Agnes.

Mrs. Waldrip shakes her head. "Young lady, I am completely lost," she says.

And Agnes is lost, too. "Didn't Joe eat poison candy?" she asks.

"What?" says Mrs. Waldrip, now looking positively horrified.

"That's what they're saying at school. And that the police came . . ."

"*Who* in the world is saying these things?" says Mrs. Waldrip. "My goodness, on top of everything else, too . . ." She takes off her gloves and runs a shaky hand across her forehead.

"Then why is Joe in the hospital?" asks Agnes.

"Joe isn't *in* the hospital," says Mrs. Waldrip. "He's there visiting." She puts her hands on her hips and mutters, "For heaven's sake."

"Oh." Agnes can't tell what kind of face she is making, exactly. And she is beginning to feel like she's intruding. "Okay," she says, "thanks."

She turns to leave and takes about three steps down the walkway when she hears: "Joe is visiting his father."

Mrs. Waldrip says this quickly and a little too loud.

Agnes looks as she puts her fingers to her lips and closes her eyes. "Dear," she says. "Come back. Please."

Agnes hesitates. "It's all right," says Mrs. Waldrip. "Come here. Sit down." Mrs. Waldrip sits on the front step and pats the space beside her. Agnes sits but leaves a big space between them.

"Now, I know you are Joe's friend," says Mrs. Waldrip. "But I can't remember your name. My mind is so boggled today. Is it Anne?"

"It's Agnes."

"That's right. Agnes." Mrs. Waldrip forces a smile. "I suppose I always just think of you as the little girl who sits on the roof."

Agnes always thought the roof was her secret place. She feels herself blushing. *To be caught snooping . . .*

"I suppose Joe told you about his mother," says Mrs. Waldrip.

"Yes," says Agnes.

"Well. It has been very difficult. For all of us."

"Oh, I know," says Agnes.

"But perhaps most especially for Joe's father," says Mrs. Waldrip. "And for me, too, because he's my son."

Mrs. Waldrip seems stuck. And so Agnes says, "I know about Joe's dad. I mean, I know he sleeps a lot."

"Yes," says Mrs. Waldrip. "Yes, that's part of it. He is very, very tired. And he was trying very hard, Agnes.

But he has a kind of sadness that makes a person sick. And if that is hard for you to understand, that's okay. Because it is hard for me, too."

"Graaaaaaaaamaaaaaaaaa!"

Both Mrs. Waldrip and Agnes turn to see Charlie shouting through the glass of the living room window.

"Can I have cookies?" He hoists a bag of Oreos up to the window and points.

"Yes!" says Mrs. Waldrip, wagging her head in an exaggerated way. "But only three." She holds up three fingers to make sure he gets the point. Charlie disappears.

"Charlie is just too young to understand what is going on," says Mrs. Waldrip. "But Joe . . ."

"Joe understands," says Agnes.

"Oh, do you think so?" says Mrs. Waldrip.

"Yeah, I do," says Agnes. "Because he knows what it's like to feel bad about his mom, too."

Suddenly, Agnes is surrounded in Mrs. Waldrip's arms. She has scooted over and pulled Agnes so close that her nose is buried in the powdery smell of Mrs. Waldrip's hair. Mrs. Waldrip is hugging so hard that her bones dig into Agnes's sides.

After a moment Agnes lifts her hand to Mrs. Waldrip's back. She pats her gently. "It's okay," she says. She can't think of anything else. And so she says it again.

Mrs. Waldrip draws back and her papery fingers

touch Agnes's cheek. "Oh no, dear. It is not okay," she says. "But that doesn't mean we're not going to keep on trying. And that someday things might be better." She lets out a deep sigh and smiles. And for the first time, Agnes sees it. Joe has Mrs. Waldrip's smile. Agnes would like to study it a while longer, but it disappears just as quickly.

"Now, dear," she says, "what were you saying about poison?"

"Don't worry about that," she says. "Someone at school was playing a . . . a joke."

"Well, it sounds like a bad joke to me," says Mrs. Waldrip.

"Yeah, it's that, all right," says Agnes.

"Joe needs a friend like you, I think." She gives Agnes's shoulder a squeeze. "Thank you, Agnes."

Agnes believes this was the absolute nicest thing that Mrs. Waldrip could say. "Oh, you're welcome," she says.

On her way home Agnes ponders. It doesn't matter anymore what Neidermeyer does or how she lies or whether she throws eggs or seventeen more dodge balls at Agnes's head. She is glad she ate that candy. It's good she did something.

She—

Agnes, Gagness, Hagness, Squanto Puker-Parker!

CHAPTER TEN

"LOOK OUT THE WINDOW, Agnes," says Mr. Parker.

"What time is it?" she asks. Agnes had been sleeping deeply, and the light seems too dim for daybreak.

"It's six a.m.," says Mr. Parker. He is always the first to get up, but usually Mrs. Parker comes in and wakes Agnes for school. "Here," he says, lifting her window curtain. "Come take a look."

Agnes throws off the covers and realizes the room is freezing. She can even see her own breath! At the window, snow is falling thick and fast in the dark morning sky, the flakes big and featherlike.

"It's a big storm," says Mr. Parker. "Looks like I'll be working at home today—"

"Dad!" says Agnes. "What about school?"

"Closed!" says Mr. Parker.

"I'm happy!" says Agnes, hugging him around the waist.

"Me, too!" says Mr. Parker.

Agnes's dad has told her that ever since he was a little boy, snow time was his favorite time. Agnes loves it, too.

She puts on an old green bathrobe and thick blue socks. Mr. Parker makes coffee while Agnes heats up some cocoa. Neither of them talk. Agnes stares out from the kitchen table at the changed backyard. A coating of snow has softened the edges of the boxwood shrubs. The patio stairs, the picnic table—all are heaped over with white. And even in the dark, the snow throws back enough light to cast a glow. If quiet had a color, thinks Agnes, it would be like this—snow glowing in the dark.

Bump! A soft snowball collides with the window just inches from where Agnes sits. Agnes looks out and sees a dark figure waving from the other side of the fence. *Joe!*

"Well, he's certainly an early bird," says Mr. Parker.

"Can he come over?" Agnes asks. "We'll just have hot chocolate and sit here and be real quiet."

Mr. Parker considers. "I suppose," he says. "As long as you let your mom sleep in."

"Yippppeeee!" Agnes whispers. She stands on her chair so Joe can get a good look at her and waves her non-cast hand over her head. Then she runs to the den to let him inside.

"Snow!" he says, when she opens the sliding glass door.

"I know!" says Agnes. "Brrrrrrr!"

Joe stamps the snow off his shoes and comes in. "It's really powdery, but you can still pack it."

"I'm dying to go out and play in it," says Agnes, "but I don't want to wake up my mom."

"Aw, come on!" says Joe. "Put your stuff on. We can go a ways down the street."

Agnes scurries upstairs and tries her best not to clomp around. It's hard enough squeezing her cast into last year's sweater. But it turns out to be impossible to fit it through the arm of her ski jacket. She tiptoes back downstairs.

"Look," she whispers. "This stupid thing won't fit over my cast!"

"Don't you have something bigger?" asks Joe.

"Yeah!" says Agnes. She creeps to the front hall closet and looks for her mother's coat. *Shoot.* It must be upstairs in her parents' bedroom. Agnes pulls down her father's big hooded parka, instead. It weighs a ton and almost falls to her ankles. But so what? The cast fits inside the sleeve without a problem.

"Don't laugh at me," says Agnes, peeking her head around the corner at Joe. She steps out. A woolen cap pulled down over her head to the top of her glasses. The sleeves of the giant parka are so long, you can't even see the tips of her mittens. To complete the look, she is wearing duck-yellow galoshes.

Joe does laugh, but not in a way that makes Agnes feel bad. "C'mon!" he says. "Snow!"

Outside, the sun has now risen, though the light is still muted. The streets are completely empty, and all Agnes can hear is the squeak and crunch of snow as they walk. Agnes sticks out her tongue to catch snowflakes. "This is just like being inside one of those shakey-uppy things," says Agnes. "You know, with the water and the plastic flakes . . ."

"Snow globes," says Joe. As he walks, he occasionally jumps up to knock a mound of snow off a tree branch or the top of a mailbox. He stops in the front yard of one house to collect snow that has gathered on top of a For Sale sign.

The house has the drapes partly open on all the first-floor windows. There is not a stick of furniture in any of the rooms. Agnes runs across the yard and presses her face to the window glass. "No one home," she says.

"Let's go look in the back!" says Joe.

The unlocked chain-link gate leads to a big flat yard—empty except for a swing set. Joe picks up a handful of snow and presses it into a ball. He lifts one eyebrow and then the other. He picks up more snow, until the snowball is the size of a small grapefruit.

"Hey! No fair!" says Agnes. "I only have one hand!"

Joe draws closer to Agnes. "I won't throw, I promise," he says. "Yet!"

"Good," says Agnes.

"But I still can . . . *smush!*" he cries, smashing the soft snowball on the top of Agnes's head.

"As much as I love being a snowball head," says Agnes as the white stuff crumbles from her cap, "I gotta tell you something. I have *always* hated snowball fights. Even when I had two good arms."

"You're kidding!" says Joe. "I thought everybody liked snowball fights."

"Nope," says Agnes.

"Well, what if I make it more fair?" He drops to his knees and makes a snowball. Then another. Soon he has a tidy little pyramid by Agnes's feet. "These are yours," he says.

Agnes reaches down and picks up a snowball. "Okay, now what?" she says.

"I'll stand here," he says, backing up about six big steps, "and you throw." Joe plants himself and stands with his hands by his sides.

Agnes stands with a snowball in hand, hesitating. "This is silly," she says.

"Have at it!" He is as serious as if he were facing a firing squad.

Agnes rolls her eyes and finally lobs a soft one at Joe's chest. Joe wobbles and then falls back, straight as a board—*thwunk!*—into the snow.

"That was *too* easy," says Agnes.

Joe sits up. "I can make it harder," he says. He stands again with his arms by his sides. "Fire away," he says.

Agnes picks up snowball number two and throws, this time a little harder. In the nick of time, however, Joe leaps to the side. It misses him by a mile. Agnes laughs and picks up snowball number three. She aims for his head. He ducks. She misses. Agnes picks up speed and starts tossing snowballs, one after the other. Joe dodges as fast as she can throw. He is just plain unhittable. "This is fun," he says.

"It is!" she yells.

Joe hops over to the swing set. He reaches up, grabs the swing chains, and lowers himself down into a seat full of snow. Agnes clomps over and takes the seat next to him, watching as he pumps his legs. He goes so high, the entire swing set starts thumping.

"You're going to tip us over!" she shrieks.

Joe whoops and lets go of the chains. *"Aaaugggghhh!"* He shoots out of the seat into the air and lands hard on his feet. Then he throws his arms up like a gymnast, smiles, and says, "Now you do it!"

"I haven't done this in a while," says Agnes.

"Don't be scared," he says.

"I'm *not* scared," says Agnes, thinking of her big clunky cast. She starts pumping with all her might.

"Higher!" Joe cries.

Now the swing is cranking and Agnes pumps until she is above Joe's shoulders.

"Go, Agnes! *Higher!*" Joe shouts.

All tangled up in the gigantic coat, Agnes gives it her very best effort. The snowflakes are collecting on her glasses, but she can tell by the way the swing drops that she is now just as high as she can go.

"Agnes—go! Now!" says Joe.

"I can't see!" yells Agnes.

"You can do it! *Jump!*" says Joe.

She does. Her rear end slips off the swing and she is blind, airborne, clutching, flying. *"Helllllp!"* she hollers. And down she goes, angling sideways. The next thing she knows, she is lying down on her good arm with her head half in the snow. She can hear the swing creaking back and forth over her head.

"Good try!" says Joe. He extends his hand and helps her up.

"Do you think so?" asks Agnes, wiping her glasses with her sleeve. She puts them back on and squints at Joe through foggy lenses. "Why are you so nice to me?" she says.

The question takes them both by surprise. "Uh, I don't know," he says.

"How can you be friends with someone like Neidermeyer," Agnes asks, "and still be friends with me?"

"What do you mean?" he says.

Even Agnes does not know exactly what she is asking. "Usually," she explains, "people sort of take sides. But you're nice to practically everybody."

"I am?" says Joe. He is looking at her as if she is speaking a language he can't understand. Then he says, "You know, Agnes, at my other school I didn't hang out with girls all the time. Is that what you mean? I'm not *trying* to do it—it's just happened for some reason . . ."

"No, I'm not even talking about that," says Agnes. "What I mean is you're nice to people who don't even deserve it."

"Oh," he says. "You mean Peggy."

"Yeah," says Agnes. She feels a little sheepish, saying that out loud.

"Peggy isn't so bad," says Joe. "You two are just different."

"What do you like about her?"

"Well, she's funny. Kind of loud. And athletic. But you're more . . . hmmm." Joe thinks hard. "You're more the quiet type."

Ugh. "Quiet?" says Agnes, trying not to show her disappointment.

"Yeah," says Joe, nudging her arm. "You know how you are . . ."

"Well maybe *Neidermeyer* should try being quiet for once," says Agnes, reddening. "She told everyone you were gone from school because you ate poisoned candy. She said the police came and you were in the hospital . . ."

Joe listens intently to the whole Neidermeyer story. He doesn't seem bothered. "Oh, you know her," he says. "She was probably mad about Halloween. It was just a joke."

"But it *wasn't* funny," says Agnes. "I was . . . a lot of us were worried . . ."

"You worried about me?" Joe says.

"Well, sure," says Agnes.

Joe is quiet. So is Agnes. Everything seems to have stopped except for the falling of snow.

"I know you talked to my grandma yesterday," Joe says.

"Yeah, I did."

"You're the only one who knows," says Joe. "The only one. Unless you told someone."

Agnes closes her eyes tight and says, "My mom." She opens one eye and peeks at Joe. "Oh, please don't be mad. I had to tell her; she's my mother. And she won't tell. Really. She promised. Do you believe me?"

Joe nods his head. He reaches down and pats the

zippered pocket of his jacket. "Can I show you something?" he says.

Agnes draws closer. Joe unzips the pocket and pulls out a key ring that has no keys on it; just a little tab of stamped leather. Agnes reaches over and takes it in her hand. The leather is printed with the initial *J.*

Joe draws himself up and points to the key chain in Agnes's hand. "I hate that thing," he says.

Agnes looks deep into her hand, trying to figure out what is so awful about this little piece of leather. "Why?" she asks.

"My dad made it," he says. "In the *mental* hospital." He holds one hand to his stomach as if the thought makes him ill. "See how it has these little flowers on it," he points out.

"Well, yeah . . ." says Agnes. "Is that bad?"

"*Yes,*" says Joe. "Before, he never would have done something like this."

"Make key chains?"

"No. He never did stuff that made me feel *sorry* for him." Joe looks over his shoulder as if he is making sure no one is listening. "If I tell you something else," he says, "will you keep it a secret?"

Agnes nods. "Yes. I swear," she says.

Joe reaches down, takes a handful of snow and packs it. "Remember when I said my dad was looking for a job?"

"Yes," says Agnes.

"Well, he wasn't. You know what he was doing?"

"No," says Agnes.

Joe winds up and hurls the snowball smack against the fence. "Nothing," says Joe. "Every day, just nothing. He parked every day at the baseball diamond and just sat there."

"Did he tell you that?" Agnes asks.

"I found him. I was on my bike, and I saw his car and, like, his feet are up on the dashboard. So I knock on the car window, he sits up and, I mean, I didn't even know what was going on until I saw his face. He looked totally wiped out. It was like *he knew* he'd been caught. He'd been doing this every day."

"Then what happened?"

"I rode off. I was really mad. Because he already told me he wouldn't come see me do my report at school. Too busy with looking for *jobs,* you know . . ." He shakes his head. "And we didn't even talk about it when he got home. I just ignored him—until he showed up at school the next day. And, uh, you know the rest . . ."

Suddenly, she doesn't like the key chain, either. She holds it out for Joe to take back.

"I don't want to keep it," he says.

"Well, what are you going to do with it?" Agnes asks.

"I don't know," he says. "I tried to carry it around,

because I thought maybe that's why he gave it to me. And I feel like I can't throw it away, you know? But I don't want it." He holds his hands up, making it impossible for Agnes to give it back.

"What should I do with it?" asks Agnes.

"Could you keep it?" he says. "Could you? Then it won't be at my house, but it won't be in the garbage, either."

"Okay," says Agnes. "If you ever want it back, just ask. I won't lose it. Promise." Joe straightens up and smiles as if he felt suddenly lighter. And, suddenly, Agnes feels better, too.

"I'll bet my grandma is making breakfast," says Joe. "Should we go back?"

"Oh, I guess so," she says. *Darn,* she thinks. On the way back, Joe jumps and hops and leaves all sorts of footprints in the snow on the sidewalk. Agnes follows and tries to land exactly in the same footprints. She misses a lot. But it is a fun game, and she keeps at it all the way to the bottom of her block.

"See ya, Agnes!" says Joe as he heads around back to his house.

"See ya, Joe!" says Agnes.

Someone is out there at the end of her own driveway, stooped over, wearing a hot-pink jacket. Agnes skips up closer and—ohmigosh. It's her dad!

Mr. Parker catches sight of Agnes. He is holding the

morning paper. "Ah, so you are the one who is responsible for my new look," he says. "I've turned into a mommy."

Agnes stares at his hot-pink parka and pajama bottoms, with his thick glasses, unshaven face, and cowlicked hair. "I think you look beautiful," she says.

CHAPTER ELEVEN

AT LAST! THINKS AGNES. This is the very last day she will ever have to take a bath with a stupid cast. No more trying to protect it with a cutoff plastic trash bag. No more sticking pencils inside to scratch the itches that have been driving her crazy. And if she ever thought lavender was a nice color, Agnes has now been cured of that completely.

"I don't know about you," says Mrs. Parker, "but I am not going to miss seeing that at the dinner table every night." Agnes knows what she means. The cast is absolutely filthy, covered in grubby doodles and scrawl. The gauze inside has frayed, turned gray, and pokes out the edges.

In the doctor's office, the nurse shows Agnes the saw she uses for removing casts. It looks like something from a miniature lumber mill. Agnes grits her teeth as the saw vibrates against the plaster and is relieved when all it does is buzz against her skin.

"See?" says the nurse. "It really doesn't hurt at all."

But the biggest surprise is seeing her arm again after all this time. It is skinny and hairy and could use a good scrubbing.

Mrs. Parker helps Agnes wash up at the big hospital sink. It has little foot pedals for hot and cold water. After several soapings and rinses, Agnes realizes that her arm is not going to get much prettier any time soon. But it is great to feel light and free and balanced again.

"Let's celebrate," says Mrs. Parker. "What would you say about going to the tearoom?"

"I would say terrific!" says Agnes. The ancient little restaurant at the very top of Lipman's Department Store has coral-colored wallpaper with murals of peach trees in bloom. All the waitresses there wear starched white caps and give you hot water in your own little silver teapot. But the best part is the ladies' room with its glittery chandeliers, marble floors, and little white hand towels that you use just once and then throw into a gold wire basket.

Mrs. Parker has told Agnes that when she was a little girl, all the young mothers used to take their daughters to the tearoom after shopping. But now when Agnes goes with her mother, they are always the youngest people there.

As they emerge from the brass-and-glass Lipman's elevator they see a large sign:

TEAROOM CLOSING AT THE NEW YEAR
OUR THANKS FOR FIFTY-FIVE WONDERFUL YEARS
LIPMAN'S MANAGEMENT

"Oh, my," says Mrs. Parker. "This just breaks my heart!"

"I know," says the waitress who shows them their seats. "I've worked here for thirty-two years."

"Such a shame," says Mrs. Parker. She spends a good while chatting with the waitress, reminiscing. By the time they place their orders, Agnes has to use the bathroom.

"I'll come with you," says Mrs. Parker. "This may be the last time I'll get to see this place."

When she and Agnes push through the ladies' room's heavy swinging door, there is a woman collapsed on the chaise lounge. She is holding a damp hand towel over her face. Agnes can see the gray curls peeking out from beneath the cloth and thinks, *Heart attack?*

"Are you all right?" asks Mrs. Parker, touching the woman gently on the shoulder.

The woman pulls the cloth from her face. She peers at Mrs. Parker and Agnes and sits upright with a jolt.

"I must look like the *silliest* old woman you have ever seen . . ." she says.

"Mrs. Waldrip!" says Agnes.

Mrs. Waldrip pushes her hair into place and straightens her skirt. "I'm supposed to meet some friends here for lunch. I haven't been out in so long," she says.

"Well, of course. You have to get out and about. Especially in this weather," says Mrs. Parker.

"Yes," says Mrs. Waldrip. "I've been experiencing the worst case of cabin fever." She glances at Agnes briefly and turns to Mrs. Parker. "I suppose you know about the troubles your neighbors are having across the fence."

"Well, yes I do," says Mrs. Parker. "It must be hard for all of you. You know, we like Joe so much. He's such a wonderful young man."

"He is, isn't he?" says Mrs. Waldrip, brightening. "And this Agnes of yours is lovely, too . . ."

Agnes gives an embarrassed smile. Should she say thank you?

"I suppose if Joe had come to stay earlier," Mrs. Waldrip continues, "I would know our younger neighbors better by now. It seems that's how you meet people, isn't it? Through the children . . ."

"Please," says Mrs. Parker, "if you ever need a place to drop off the boys, call me. Even if you just want to go grocery shopping by yourself. We would be delighted to have them over."

Mrs. Waldrip's face softens. "Well, I do appreciate that. So much. Do you know you are the first person who has offered to help?"

Agnes's mother sits down next to Mrs. Waldrip. Agnes sees her tilt her head in that way she has that makes you want to tell her everything. "You must feel so overwhelmed," says Mrs. Parker.

Mrs. Waldrip peeks to see that no one can overhear her. Then she says in a low voice, "Every single thing in my life has changed. I do think that a mere breeze could just send me over the edge. And, oh, you are going to think I'm batty . . ."

"I certainly will not," says Mrs. Parker.

"When I saw that the tearoom is closing, well, it felt like the last straw. I became . . . so dizzy." Mrs. Waldrip touches her forehead. "What I wouldn't give for an aspirin right now."

Mrs. Parker reaches into her purse. "Agnes, would you please go back to our table and get Mrs. Waldrip a glass of water?"

"Sure," says Agnes. She is relieved to be given something to do. And a chance to move around, because she really needs to use the bathroom now. In the tearoom, Agnes looks to see which table Mrs. Waldrip might be joining. It is a tearoom full of Mrs. Waldrips. There aren't many places like this anymore for ladies like her—*outside of church,* thinks Agnes.

She returns with a sweating glass of ice water. Now Mrs. Waldrip and Mrs. Parker are laughing and the entire mood in the ladies' lounge has changed. Agnes wonders if she'll ever be able to do what her mother does: Come in, say the right thing, and make everyone feel better.

True to her promise, Mrs. Parker arranges to take Charlie and Joe after school on Tuesdays and Thursdays for as long as Mrs. Waldrip needs it. Joe's father will be back home that week for Thanksgiving; but even then, everyone agrees it would be best to take it easy on him for a while.

Today is the first Tuesday. Agnes will have Joe over for almost three whole hours. He will walk home with her, too!

The sun has made an appearance in a completely blue sky. If it weren't for the slush on the ground, it might be late spring. "Please, please, please, Mrs. Libonati!" says Brian. "Can we play baseball today?"

"Why, Brian, I'm surprised at you," says Libbo. "Are you sure you wouldn't like another nice quiet indoor recess? I ran off some word puzzles and everything."

Brian hesitates. Mrs. Libonati has made an actual joke!

"Oh, okay," she says. "Why not? Baseball it is."

"Yay!" holler the kids. It is a slow-moving, slippery game, but nobody seems to mind. Neidermeyer is so absorbed in making strategies for her own team, she doesn't even jeer when Agnes drops the ball on a pop fly.

Neidermeyer has, in fact, been less, well—Neidermeyer-ish these last few weeks. Although she never apologized for starting the rumor about Joe, Agnes notices that she is more careful—especially in Joe's presence. And there is altogether less arm socking and taunting. Even Carmella has caught on. She looks bewildered sometimes, tagging along quietly at her hero's elbow.

Agnes has not managed to tell Prejean about Joe coming over twice a week. Or that she plans on walking home with him on those days, too. She waits until after school, when she and Prejean are walking down the hall. Nervous, Agnes is walking straight as a board and clapping her hands at her sides like a penguin.

"You're acting all nutty," says Prejean.

Agnes stops flapping just as she sees Joe come out of the classroom door. "Look," she says to Prejean. "Joe's coming home to my house. His little brother, too. Every Tuesday and Thursday. And I'm going to walk with him, and I know that is going to make you really mad."

Prejean opens her mouth to speak.

"*But* I'm going to do it anyway," continues Agnes. "Because I like him and there's nothing wrong with it and *it's okay to have more than one friend!*"

"Okay," says Prejean, whispering through clenched teeth. She gives Agnes an exaggerated *look-who's-behind-you* look. "I *get* it."

Agnes wheels around. "Hey, Joe," she says, hoping he hasn't been there long.

"I have to pick up Charlie," says Joe. "He's waiting at the kindergarten bungalow."

"And I gotta get on home," says Prejean. "See ya." She waves and runs off.

"See ya!" Agnes calls after her. *Oh, why does this all have to be so complicated?*

When Joe and Agnes catch up with Charlie, he is holding on to the flagpole with one hand and walking around in circles. He stops, looks at them, and says, "Where's Peggy?"

"We're going over to Agnes's today," says Joe.

"But where's Peggy?" he says again.

"Peggy went home with Carmella," says Joe.

"Oh," says Charlie.

"Anyway, what do you care?" says Joe. "I don't think you've ever said one word to her."

Charlie walks with his head hung down. "I like to watch her," he says.

Agnes's mind races ahead. Today is like a test. Everything has to be perfect.

"Charlie," says Agnes, "how would you like to play a game on my computer?"

"What game?" says Charlie.

"It's a game about a car that goes to the moon," says Agnes. It was her favorite computer game when she was little.

Charlie thinks it over. "Nah," he says.

"Then how about . . . something funner?" suggests Agnes. "Um, do you like to play pretend? We could be bad guys or pirates and you could . . ."

Charlie shakes his head back and forth. "Nah," he says.

"Oh, I got it! Let's climb trees!" says Agnes. "Yeah! We'll climb the big, scary, tall ones down at the short-cut woods—"

"*What?*" Joe looks at Agnes as if he might start laughing.

"I climb trees, Joe," says Agnes defensively. "I do!"

"How about TV, Charlie?" asks Joe.

"Yeah," Charlie says.

"See? He's easy." Joe smiles.

"But TV is so nothing," says Agnes. Come to think of it, she has never seen Charlie do anything but watch cartoons and eat cookies. He doesn't seem to care for any sort of games. "I'll bet you were different when you were little," says Agnes.

"Well, yeah. My dad played ball with me a lot," says Joe. "You know, catch, sports, stuff like that. My mom, too."

At her house Agnes takes everyone's backpack and throws them in the front hall closet. She stares into the dark for a few moments, and then says, "You know what? I want to play hide-and-go-seek! And I think we can get Charlie to play, too," she says. "We'll just promise him a cookie every time he finds one of us . . ."

"Yep. He'll go for that," says Joe.

Joe has to nag a little to get Charlie to play. But the possibility of getting cookies out of the game finally gets him off the couch.

"You have to close your eyes while we hide. Can you count to twenty?" Agnes asks Charlie.

Charlie scowls. "I can count to a hundred," he says.

Oops. As he starts to count, Agnes and Joe scatter. Agnes heads for the front hall closet. She manages to get the door shut but has trouble finding a place for her feet. The floor is crammed with backpacks. At first she tries shoving them aside with kicks.

Then, reaching down in the dark, she finds a pack and props it in the corner. *That's better.* Then she fishes around, finds another backpack, and grabs it by the bottom. When she lifts it, she hears a clatter of stuff: pencils, change, and who-knows-what else. *Rats.* She stands on tiptoe until she can feel the hanging lightbulb chain and gives it a pull.

The spilled backpack is Joe's! She scoops up some dimes and a couple of nickels and puts them neatly in a little side pocket. There is a flat round eraser that looks like a soccer ball, a pencil without a point . . . And beneath her heel, another pencil, this one with bite marks in the center. Agnes traces the dents with her finger. *Could I keep this?* She also manages to locate a plastic protractor, crumpled foil and NBA cards from a pack of gum, and an erasable pen.

And just as she is about to reach up and turn off the light again, she spots something else. Agnes picks it up. It is a piece of notebook paper folded into quarters. The handwriting is not Joe's. It is fat and messy and written with one of those big blunt pencils. Agnes opens it up flat, feeling so guilty and sneaky, she has to calm herself to hold it steady.

> *Joe:*
>   *First I said bunt and you ignored it. You know
> I was right with Brian on second and Jay in right
> field but you did it on purpose. Then you tell me
> your walking home with HAGNESS. You will prob-
> ably just throw this note in the trash.*
> *P.N.*
>
> *P.S. If your mad ok. If you can't take a joke ok.
>   Maybe you think it is a big joke if some one said
>   I love you. I wouldn't dout it.*
> *P.P.S. I'm sorry.*

Agnes wants to drop the note, wants to release it from her hands as soon as possible. But she can't. She reads it again and again. " . . . *If someone said I love you . . .*" *Ick* . . . Neidermeyer is—in love!

The thought of writing the word *love* on a paper and having him read it! The thought of *saying* the word *love* out loud in front of him . . .

"Gotcha!"

The closet door swings open. Standing there are Charlie and Joe. Agnes is frozen, holding the note in both hands. Her eyes meet Joe's. He blinks once. And then he turns on his heel and walks away.

Agnes fishes in her pocket for Charlie's cookie. She is hot and trembling with shame. Charlie takes the cookie and runs off.

Agnes emerges slowly from the closet. She walks down the hall and peeks into the den. Charlie is sitting in front of the TV. "Do you know where Joe is?" Agnes asks.

"He left," says Charlie.

"Where?"

Charlie points toward the direction of the backyard. The sliding glass door is still open.

She walks out to patio. *He's gone.*

CHAPTER TWELVE

"I DON'T WANT TO GO TO SCHOOL."

These are the first words out of Agnes's mouth when she wakes up, and she is saying them to the ceiling.

In the hallway Mrs. Parker is on the phone with Mrs. Waldrip. "Well, of course, Edna," says Mrs. Parker. "That would be fine," she says. She hangs up and calls to Agnes. "Honey, Mrs. Waldrip wants us to know that Joe is going to Peggy Neidermeyer's on Tuesdays and Thursdays."

"Oh," said Agnes, wishing even harder that she could fall back into bed with a thud.

"Is anything wrong?" she asks.

"Nope, Neidermeyer is his best friend," says Agnes

as a little punishment to herself. *I made Joe hate me*, thinks Agnes. *I told him "You can trust me. I won't tell anyone. I promise, I promise . . ."* And now all she has are these waves of sadness. It is as if all the good things had been erased.

If only she could go back in time, or skip today and go directly to tomorrow: Thanksgiving, followed by three whole days of vacation. Altogether, Joe would have four whole days to be less mad or hurt or both.

Agnes tries to think of something she can offer Joe. Something that will express how deeply, sincerely sorry she is. She slides out of bed and goes to the jewelry box she keeps on top of her dresser. When she opens the lid, a plastic ballerina pops up. She picks up one of Prejean's tiny, shiny baby teeth. There are also some pins her mother earned as a little girl in Brownies. These things are precious to Agnes. But they wouldn't mean anything to Joe.

The morning weather matches her mood. Sluggish gray clouds have moved in overnight. Yesterday's slush has refrozen. It would be easier to get through the day if only she could stay in her fat warm jacket with a scarf wrapped halfway around her face. But Libbo wouldn't stand for that, so Agnes takes her snow things off in the coatroom with all the others.

"You look tired," says Prejean.

"I feel *blecch*," says Agnes.

"Why?" Prejean asks.

"I did something I should never have done." Agnes tosses her boots in a corner a little harder than she intended. They make a loud *thud*.

"Are you okay?"

Agnes looks at Prejean's face with the soft brown eyes and the three wrinkles that always appear on her forehead when she's curious. "Oh, Prejean!" she says with sudden feeling. "Can't we just go back to the way everything was before? I just want to play at your house and watch Tiff and Zori and talk on the pink plastic phone."

"You do?"

"Yeah. Just you and me together." Agnes tells her about everything—Neidermeyer and the note. "So, see?" she says. "I'm back. Your old regular Agnes. And I'm going to be free every Tuesday and Thursday for the rest of my life." She smiles sadly. "Good news, huh?"

"Oh . . ." says Prejean. "But, Agnes . . ."

"What?" Agnes shrugs. "I thought you'd be happy."

"You're not even going to try to apologize to him or anything?" says Prejean. "Ever?"

"Not if he stays mad at me," says Agnes flatly.

"But he can't stay mad!" says Prejean.

"Why not?"

"Because," says Prejean, "it's just not *fair*, that's why."

All day Agnes waits to see what Joe will do when he sees her. But he never does see her. He never gets up to sharpen his pencil. And he spends indoor recess playing a game of Risk with Brian, Neidermeyer, and Carmella. Everywhere, even at lunch, Joe will not sit facing Agnes.

When the last bell rings, Agnes rushes to put on her jacket and scarf. She sees Joe heading for the door. She is shaky and hot-faced and fumbling with her mittens, when he looks behind him, raises his hand, and waves. Agnes raises her hand, too. Her heart is nearly bursting with hope when she feels a bump on the shoulder. Neidermeyer pushes on past.

"I'm coming, Joe!" Neidermeyer shouts. She bounds up to the doorway and socks Joe in the arm. They both turn their backs as the door closes behind them. Agnes realizes that her arm is still up, paralyzed in mid-wave.

It is Thanksgiving, and Nana Parker is snowed in 350 miles away. Agnes's aunt Joanna is spending the holiday at Uncle Tim's parents' home. Because there are only three of them this year, Mrs. Parker has fixed a chicken instead of a turkey. Agnes finds this unforgivable. She picks at her plate.

"How's the chicken?" asks Mrs. Parker.

"Mmmmmm," says Mr. Parker.

"Tastes chickeny," says Agnes pointedly.

After dinner, in the moonless dark, the Parkers take their annual drive down Peacock Lane. Every Thanksgiving at seven o'clock, the Christmas lights go on at Peacock Lane for the first time. It is a big event always featured on the local news.

"Well, this makes it official," says Mrs. Parker. "The holiday season has begun!"

Agnes knows that her mother has turned around to smile at her, so she hunkers down in her seat and stares out the window. Hundreds of people have shown up tonight. Blocks before they reach the lit-up houses, cars snake slowly through the streets. Each car in the long line idles, softly breathing exhaust, its taillights making the snow glow red. Mrs. Parker puts in a tape. Bing Crosby sings a song about being home for Christmas.

Agnes cannot listen to Bing Crosby sing without picturing an old bassett hound, wet-eyed and saggy-faced, warbling into a microphone. She wants to ask her mother to change the music but knows that nothing would actually cheer her up. Better to sit silent and just continue feeling horrible.

And then Mrs. Parker puts her hand on Mr. Parker's shoulder and softly sings: "Christmas Eve will find me where the love light gleams . . ." She continues the song, her hand tracing his neck and resting on his cheek. Agnes's dad smiles back almost shyly, and Agnes can see how nutty he still is about her very own mother. She keeps watching them out of the corner of her eye, in spite of herself.

"I'll be home for Christmas—if only in my dreams," sings Bing Crosby just as the car rounds the corner onto Peacock Lane. "*Ahh,* beautiful," says Mrs. Parker. And it truly is. The rows of steep-roofed houses are ablaze with colored lights and frosty snow. The oaks that line the street look hung with sparkling crystal and powdered sugar. Agnes's dad leans toward her mom and kisses her lightly on the lips.

"Geez," says Agnes.

"Are we old people embarrassing you?" Mrs. Parker asks.

Agnes shakes her head no, even though they are. She can't help but think, as she watches Mrs. Parker resting her head on her husband's shoulder, how nice, how easy, it must be to be a grown-up.

In the morning Agnes looks out the little window above her dresser. It is such a perfect picture frame for the Waldrips' backyard. Smoke curls from the Waldrips' chimney, and Agnes wonders if Joe's dad built the fire. At that moment Mrs. Waldrip emerges from the back of the garage. She is wearing her heavy plaid coat and is carrying a plastic bag. Birdseed. She pours some into the hands of the statue of St. Francis and scatters some more on the snow.

Agnes can hear her mother outside below her window. "Good morning," calls Mrs. Waldrip. She stands on a picnic bench and waves Mrs. Parker over to the fence. Agnes leans so close to the window, her breath keeps clouding the view. It is impossible to hear anything the two women are saying, but she does make out the look on Mrs. Waldrip's face.

Agnes is waiting for her mother when she returns from the backyard. "What did she say?" Agnes asks. "Is everything all right?"

"I'm not sure, but I hope so," says her mother.

"What do you mean?"

"She said Joe's dad is taking the kids and going back home."

"They're *leaving*?"

"Yes," says Mrs. Parker. "Next week."

The news feels like a slap. "Why?" says Agnes.

"I really don't know, honey," says Mrs. Parker. "I guess it's something Joe's dad decided when he was in the hospital. He just told his family about it yesterday."

Did Joe decide that the kids here are such creeps, he asked his dad if they could move? Agnes knows this is silly and tries to think more clearly. Gosh, the thought of him moving is bad enough; but the thought of him leaving while still mad at her is, well, unbearable. Unthinkable.

And then she says out loud, "I just want him to be happy. Even if he has to go away. That's okay, as long as he's happy."

"I feel the same way," says Mrs. Parker. "It would be

so nice if life would just give that family a break." She strokes the top of Agnes's hair. Agnes thinks about how good it would be if Joe had a mom to do this for him. Joe, crowded in that bedroom with all the stuff from their old life. And those boxes, piled against the wall, all with bits and pieces of his mom's things.

She feels the clouds pressing down on her head begin to lift. There are three remaining vacation days. Agnes leaps to her feet. "I've got to get started on something!" she says to her mother.

The next Monday morning at school starts out with an astonishing sight—Neidermeyer sitting at her desk facedown, with her head in her arms. The rumor is that Libbo has just given her a blue slip that her parents must sign. And today, she has detention after school.

"I wasn't here," says Prejean, "but Ashley says Neidermeyer kicked over a trash can. And she was *crying.*"

Nobody has ever seen Neidermeyer cry. Agnes tries hard to catch a glimpse of her, but her head is glued to her forearms. After almost fifteen minutes of this, Mrs. Libonati turns from the blackboard and says, "Peggy, it's time to sit up." She says it firmly, and even Neidermeyer knows she is going to have to comply.

The eyes of the whole class turn upon Neidermeyer as she lifts her head, crosses her arms, and slides down in her seat. Agnes cranes her neck a little for a better look. Wet eyelashes and a splotchy face. Peggy Neidermeyer looks just like any other girl who has been crying.

Somehow, Agnes doesn't feel that good about seeing her this way. She feels embarrassed for Neidermeyer. Maybe even sorry?

"Neidermeyer likes *Joe*!" Brian whispers to Agnes.

"So?" says Agnes.

"So this is his last day of school," says Brian. "She's, like, having a nervous breakdown."

"Brian," says Agnes, "are you sure this is Joe's last day?"

"Definitely. He told me," says Brian.

Agnes looks down the next row to spot Joe's red plaid shirt. He is bent over his desk writing, holding his pencil with his little kidlike, awkward grip. *Oh, Joe.*

"That does it," Prejean says to Agnes at morning recess. "He's leaving and you have to say something."

"I was going to, but now there isn't enough time," says Agnes.

"Yes, there is," insists Prejean.

"No, no, no. I can tell he's still mad at me."

"So what?" says Prejean. "Are you never supposed to make a mistake? Don't you still love me, even when I act like a bozo?" She puts her hands on her hips. "You are a great friend to have, Agnes Parker. And you should know that about yourself!"

This remark stops Agnes. "Prejean," she says. "That's so . . . so nice of you."

"Yeah," says Prejean. "And I swear we are not going to let Joe Waldrip leave before he knows it, too."

"*You* are going to help *me* with Joe?" And Agnes doesn't dare say so, but she can't get over how much Prejean really *is* exactly like her mother!

Prejean bites her lip. Her eyes roll up as if she is looking inside her own head for ideas. And she finds something! She makes Agnes promise to do exactly what she says: "Go home after school and wait."

At the last bell, all Agnes does is glance over at Prejean to say good-bye. *"Shoo!"* she says. She scoots her off with her hands. Her friend means business. Agnes obeys.

The afternoon clouds are sifting down the most perfect snowflakes. When Agnes catches them on her navy blue mittens, she can count all six points on most flakes. She blows on them and watches them disappear. She keeps doing this even though it makes her sad.

When she enters her front door, Agnes doesn't call to her mother or take off her coat. Instead, she sits on the den sofa in all her snow things and waits. Finally, she clicks on the television. An audience is clapping for a person who is making fresh fruit juice.

Agnes watches the bulky plastic machine suck the juice from an apple. The audience explodes with cheers and more applause. Then, one by one, carrots are fed into the machine. *Splurt. Splurt.* Muddy orange juice splats from the machine's little hose.

What am I doing? she thinks. She raises the remote control and the television clicks off. She stands to take off her coat, when . . . standing only a few feet away outside the sliding glass door, is Joe.

He is standing with his hands in his pockets. She can only put her hand to her mouth and stare. Finally a little voice in her head says, *Oh, come on, Agnes. Let him in!*

"You're here," says Agnes.

"Yeah," says Joe.

"I'm sorry," says Agnes.

"I know," says Joe.

"I should *never* have read that note. Never. It fell out of your backpack accidentally, but I shouldn't have looked at it . . . and I'm really, *really* sorry."

"Well, it just didn't seem like something someone like *you* would do," says Joe. "You know?"

"Yeah, I didn't expect it of me either, exactly."

"And after all that stuff I told you . . ." says Joe.

"I know. It was so, so wrong," says Agnes. "I've been walking around for days just wishing there was a way to show you . . . I mean, if there were some way you could look inside me and *see,* you'd know. You really can trust me. I swear you can."

"That's what Prejean said," says Joe.

Thank you, thank you, Prejean, thinks Agnes.

"But I knew it anyway. *Everyone* knows it. I was just mad."

Everyone? Agnes has never thought about everyone thinking anything about her at all.

"I hear you have something for me," he says.

Agnes says, "Yeah. It's upstairs. Want to come with me?"

Joe follows Agnes to her room. He looks out the little window. "Man, you can see everything from here."

"I haven't seen you, not for days," says Agnes. "I've been watching."

"We've been doing a lot of packing," says Joe.

"Why do you have to go now?" asks Agnes.

"It's my dad's idea. He wants us back home by Christmas. We have to find another house. He thinks it will be easier if we have some time to get settled before we go back to our old school."

"What does Charlie think?" she asks.

"He's glad," says Joe. "He wants things like they used to be."

"And what do you think?" asks Agnes.

"I think . . . some things change forever."

"Yes," says Agnes. "I guess they do." She goes over to her desk and picks up a little cardboard box. "This is for you," says Agnes.

Joe smiles. He reaches in the box and pulls out a metal ring dangling with cutout pieces of paper.

"It's your key chain," says Agnes. "But I changed it. I took off your dad's leather thing, and I put keys on it. See? There are five keys, and they all have a wish for you. For when you move back," she says.

Joe looks at the first key. It has holly drawn on it with red berries made of glitter. "'A Very Merry Christmas,'" he reads.

"I hope you like it," says Agnes.

Joe reads the next key. "'Old Friends,'" he says.

"That's from Girl Scouts," says Agnes. "There is a song about old friends and new friends. New friends are silver and the old ones are gold."

"Oh," says Joe. "So that's what this silver one is for?"

Agnes nods. "And the red one is for your family. It is a wish that you'll be happy together."

"What about the purple one?" he asks.

"Um, that's lavender," says Agnes. "It stands for me."

"What's the wish?" says Joe.

"It's really my wish," says Agnes, feeling her blush turn to a burn. "I wish that you will come see me when you visit your grandmother."

"Thanks," says Joe. He puts the key chain back in the box. "I won't lose it." He says this as if he were swearing to keep a secret or putting his hand on a Bible or saying the Pledge of Allegiance. They both keep their eyes fixed on the key ring for a moment.

"I gotta go, Agnes," he says. "Grandma is taking us out for steak and we have to dress up." He cocks his head. "You want to walk me home?"

"Yeah," says Agnes.

As they walk through every room, Agnes thinks: *We're leaving my room. We're leaving my stairs. We're leaving my hallway* . . . She is trying to break the goodbye down into little pieces so it will be less enormous.

Now they're walking through the backyard snow. Then Agnes watches him climb over the fence. "Goodbye, Joe!" she says. Just when she thinks he is gone forever, she hears Joe's voice once more. "Hey, c'mere," he says.

Agnes looks closely and sees a finger sticking through the knothole of the fence. She dares to touch it. She and Joe are hooking fingers.

"You're the best, Agnes," he says.

I tried, she thinks. And she is so glad she did.

"I'll be back," he says.

Agnes rests her forehead against the rough wood. "Good," she says. She loosens her grasp and Joe's finger slips away.

Agnes turns away from the fence. She gazes on the lines of footprints Joe made between her house and his. *He came and he went, just like that.* She sits on her knees and touches one of the tracks. The pattern of his shoe, two circles surrounded by diamonds, is already turning fuzzy in the falling snow.

I will sit right here all night and shield it from the flakes, she thinks.

It's a nice thought. Another wish, actually. She holds on to it for a moment longer, and then lets it go.

KATHLEEN O'DELL cites the acclaimed author Beverly Cleary as a source of comfort and inspiration throughout her life. As she read Cleary's books, Kathy wondered how the author could possibly know so much about *her*.

Agnes Parker . . . Girl in Progress was born of Kathy's memories of many of her own experiences, especially those drawn from a time when "my feelings, my friends, and my world were changing so fast." Like Agnes, she broke her arm and got glasses. And, also like Agnes, she still considers herself and her life to be an ever-changing project, one shared with her husband, Tim, and their children, Sam and Charlie. They live in Glendale, California. Kathy is also the author of *Ophie Out of Oz* and *Agnes Parker...Happy Camper?*